# MICAH

*A Demons-In-Law Novel*

## LOUISA MASTERS

Micah

Copyright © 2023 by Louisa Masters

Cover: Booksmith Design

Illustrated Paperback Cover Art: Christine Marie

Editor: Hot Tree Editing

All rights reserved.

No part of this book may be reproduced in any form or by any means without the prior written consent of the author, excepting brief quotes used in reviews.

This is a work of fiction. Names, characters, places, events and incidents either are the product of the author's imagination or are used fictitiously, and any resemblance to persons, living or dead, business establishments, events or locales is entirely coincidental.

To the extent that the image or images on the cover of this book depict a person or persons, such person or persons are merely models and are not intended to portray any character or characters featured in the book.

# MICAH

*Wanted: Demon assistant for incubus genius. Personal services required...*

Nobody ever expected to find a secret cave protected by a giant puzzle door in the mountains near our village. Even more surprising was the knowledge that it's been there for thousands of years and was created by a dragon. I'm not the only one who's dying to find out what's inside.

It's no hardship to assist the puzzle expert who's coming to solve the door. That thing is an incredible feat of engineering, and the man who'll solve it is bound to be intelligent and interesting. But from the moment I meet Camden Torrence, I'm forced to reassess... everything.

He's intelligent and interesting, sure. But he's also scattered. Clumsy. And I want to bury my face in his mop of curls and stay there forever.

A relationship wasn't on my agenda, no matter what my matchmaking family wants. But as the weeks go by and we get closer to discovering what the secret treasure is, Cam becomes an integral, undeniable part of my life. How can I not fall for a man who, despite past hurts, is the living embodiment of sunshine in our snow-laden village?

I never thought the love of my life would turn out to be an adorable, absent-minded incubus, but now I can't imagine existing without him. The challenge? Convincing him to stay even after the puzzle is solved.

# CHAPTER ONE

## Cam

I stare at the photos again, every fiber of my being aching to get my hands on that puzzle. It's... incredible. Gorgeous.

*Soon.*

That's what I've been telling myself for the last two weeks, but this time it's more true than it's ever been before. I'm literally right now waiting for the demon who's supposed to be taking me to my pretty, pretty puzzle.

Or rather... *their* pretty puzzle. It's not mine, dammit. I'm not entirely sure who it belongs to. Alistair, the friend who hooked me up with this job, wasn't all that clear on those details, just that it's in a mountain cave in the Swiss Alps and I'll be hosted by the closest town. Or maybe he did tell me, and I wasn't paying attention because my brain was overloaded by the contents of the pictures he sent me.

The pictures of a twenty-foot-high, twenty-foot-wide mechanical puzzle door. And they want me to unlock it for them.

I've never said yes to anything so fast in my life. If they hadn't asked, I would have begged them to let me come see it... and play with it.

*Soon.*

The two weeks it took me to finish up some client commissions and move things around dragged out forever. I'm super proud of myself for not tossing it all aside and telling Alistair I could come immediately. I wanted to, but if I want to keep this very comfortable life designing and building custom puzzles for commission clients, I need to not piss them all off by making them wait longer than promised. Lucky for me, puzzles are my work and my joy, and I'd rather be messing around with them than watching TV in the evenings, so I'm always slightly ahead of schedule. As long as I'm back to work in two months, everything will be fine. And unless that wall/door has some very big (and exciting) secrets, it won't take me half that time to solve it. That gives me plenty of time to play with it and study it. Maybe I'll even be able to track down the designer! I'd love to talk to them.

A message notification pops up on my phone, partially blocking the picture of the pretty, and I swipe it away, annoyed. It's quickly followed by another, and I sigh and switch over to the message app.

UNKNOWN CONTACT:

think you can hide from me?

im coming for you muthafucka

Ugh. Not this again. I consider messaging back to correct his spelling and punctuation, but honestly, I'm sick of getting these messages, and me replying just makes him send more. What kind of idiot orders a custom commission product, tries to cheat the vendor by filing a chargeback but is too stupid to wait until *after* it's shipped, then contacts that same vendor raging about how I never sent it? Of course I never sent it; you tried to steal it from me.

I was so outraged by his audacity that I sent all our correspondence to the credit card company, making it clear that I was happy for the charge to be canceled, since I still had the product, but that the chargeback claim was fraudulent. I felt petty about it after, until my accountant told me that chargebacks can impact my merchant reputation with the bank and credit companies.

Unfortunately, the client—his name is Cary Mack—seems to have taken it all personally, and the threatening emails started soon after that. Then he somehow found my phone number, and the texts started. He really needs to find a hobby. I'd suggest mechanical puzzles, but that might be like salt in a wound, since I certainly won't sell him one.

The doorbell peals through the house, and my whole body lights up with excitement. He's here! The demon who's going to take me to the pretty has *finally* arrived. I hope we can go straight there and not have to bother with any official bullshit.

I grab my suitcase with all my work gear—the pictures show some light rust on the door, so I decided it would be smart to bring tools in case repairs were needed—and the overnight bag with my clothes and shit. I hope there's a washer there for me to use, or I'm gonna run out of underwear real quick. It should be fine. Alistair would have told me if I needed to be prepared for irregular conditions.

Hmm. Maybe he did, and I just wasn't listening?

Oh well. I'll find out soon.

I drag my stuff toward the front door—tools are fucking heavy—and accidentally bump into the hall table, knocking the key bowl to the floor with a clatter.

"Fuck," I mutter. Although, maybe it's a good thing. I'm about 99.99 percent sure I was about to forget my keys. "Coming!" I call, not wanting the demon—shit, did Alistair tell me his name?—to get impatient and leave. Demons aren't known for their patience.

I can hear voices, so maybe he brought a friend. I've never teleported with a demon before—maybe we needed another person to teleport my bags.

Scooping up the bowl and my keys, I dump everything back on the table, pick up my overnight bag, drag everything three more steps, stop, drop my bags, go back for my keys—dammit—and then finally manage to get myself and my stuff to the door. I fling it open and say, "Hi!" to the back of a man's head.

Huh. The back of his head is nice enough, as those things go, with thick dark hair in a neat style, but it wasn't what I was expecting. Why's he staring—

Tires squeal, and a car peels off down the street. I glance after it, then back to my... visitor? Guide? Transportation facilitator? Why does he care so much about that car? It's not his, is it? Did someone steal his car?

No, he teleported here. From Switzerland. Where he's going to take me just as soon as he stops being so distracted.

"Uh... hello?"

He turns to face me finally, and I take a step back at the mean-looking frown on his face. Whoa. Not friendly. It's too bad, because he's seriously *fiiiiine*. I like attractive men, even the straight ones. People lust after them, and that generates plenty of sexual energy to keep me healthy. That's why I live in this neighborhood, even though it's a bit iffy. There are three strip clubs within a two-block radius, and that means lots of residual sexual energy for those times when I get caught up in work and forget I need sustenance.

"Camden?" he asks. "Are you Camden Torrence?"

"Cam," I correct. Nobody calls me Camden.

"Were you expecting someone? A visitor?"

It's my turn to frown, and I hesitate. Is he not my ride? He's a demon—I can tell, even though he has his horns glamoured to hide them from humans. Those of us in the community don't need physical characteristics to recognize each other.

"I was expecting someone... is that not you? Because I'm all ready to go." I gesture to my bags and somehow drop my keys. "Whoops."

When I straighten from picking them up, he's staring at me. "Do I have something on my face?" I swipe at my cheek and only just avoid putting my eye out with my keys. Maybe there's a machine oil smudge. Working with moving metal bits calls for it, and sometimes I'm not as neat as I could be.

"No, there's nothing on your face. I... There was a man at your door. He'd just knocked. But when I got here and said hi, he ran off. That was him in the car, driving like he'd been set on fire."

"Oh. Well, hopefully he slows down before he causes an accident," I say brightly. "Are we ready to go?"

The frown comes back as he studies my face. "Aren't you curious? Or concerned? This isn't exactly the safest neighborhood in the world." He pointedly glances at the overgrown yards with cars up on blocks, and the group of young men hanging out on a porch across the street. My yard isn't overgrown, but only because it's concreted. Not by me—the previous owner did it—but it was a definite selling point when I bought the place. One less thing for me to forget to take care of.

I shrug. "Meh. I'm not gonna be here, and I'm bringing my tools with me. There's not really anything else worth stealing." Not unless the thief wants some bolts and other bits of metal. I work on commission only, so I don't have any finished pieces in the house, just components.

He blinks. "But... it's still not good for someone to break into your home. What if they decide to stick around once they realize you're not here? They could wait for you to come back."

And then what? Ransom me off? Nobody's paying money for me. The only value I'd have to them is if they want a custom mechanical puzzle, which seems like a stretch.

But this guy doesn't seem like he's gonna let this go, and I really want to leave. So I smile confidently at him and put down my bags. "You're right. I should take precautions for while I'm gone." Stepping past him, I cup my hands around my mouth and shout, "Hey, Lenny! I'm going away for a bit. Keep an eye on the house for me?"

One of the men across the street looks up. He and his friends do stuff I don't ask questions about, ever, but they've been nice to me ever since I moved in and gave Lenny's daughter a puzzle. He's super proud of her, says she's going to be a scientist one day.

"I gotcha, man," he calls back, then glares at my new friend... demon teleporter guy.

My new friend glares right back. I guess it takes more than a drug dealer to intimidate a demon. Or maybe he's like Alistair, trained to kill in a million different ways.

I wave my thanks, then turn back to the house. "All set."

He seems to be on the verge of saying something, then changes his mind and nods. "Sure. All set." He looks down at my bags. "Uh, I'm not sure how we're gonna do this with your neighbors watching."

"We can go inside," I suggest.

"Yeah, but you just told them you were going away. And your bags are here. They're going to expect you to actually *leave*."

Oh. Good point. "Let's take my bags and walk down the block. There are a few shady alleys we can duck into. Nobody looks down them, because sometimes it's best not to see things."

From the expression of distaste on his face, he doesn't live in a neighborhood like mine. What a Judgy McJudgerson.

"Sounds... great." He reaches down and picks up the suit-case, then makes a pained sound. "What exactly is in here?"

"Tools." I grab my overnight bag. "But it has wheels."

"I need to get it down the steps," he points out. "What kind of tools?"

I jump down the aforementioned steps. "Ones I use to work. I'm not sure if I'll need them, but better safe than sorry!"

"Funny how that approach applies to your work but not your house or your person," he mutters, not moving from the porch. "Does the door lock automatically?"

"No. Why?"

He tilts his head toward my front door... which is still open. Damn.

"Whoops!" I jog up the four steps, pull it closed, then lock it. It only takes me two tries, and I don't drop the keys *at all*. Go me. "Okay, now we're ready." I turn back to the steps, and my cranky travel buddy sighs and reaches past me to pull my keys out of the lock.

Even for me, that's ridiculous, but I'm not telling him that.

# CHAPTER TWO



## Micah

This can't be real. I'm being pranked—that must be it. Garrett and his cousin are pulling one of those pranks hellhounds love so much. I've heard about them, even if I haven't been around hellhounds enough to have been the victim of one before. Maybe the humans across the street who look like they eat their own young for funsies are also in on it.

Because the expert who specializes in mechanical puzzles —who's going to solve the incredibly intricate feat of design and engineering that my cousins and I discovered last month —cannot possibly be the same guy who seems incapable of walking down the street without hurting himself or leaving a trail of belongings behind him.

Except he definitely is.

Sighing, I drag his heavy-as-a-pile-of-rocks suitcase down his front steps and gesture for him to lead the way. "I'm Micah, by the way. Micah Bailey."

He stops so suddenly, I nearly run into him, then spins around, the overnight bag on his shoulder tumbling to the ground as he holds out his hand. "Nice to meet you! Thanks so much for coming to get me. I've never traveled this way before, but it's got to be better than endless hours on a plane." He wrinkles his nose, and I can't say I blame him. I've never been on a plane before—why would I?—but the thought of being enclosed in a metal tube with hundreds of other people and recycled air for hours... well, it doesn't sound fun. Teleporting is clearly the best form of transport.

Although recently I learned that some of the elves can use portals for travel that are just like a doorway. So while *I* still prefer teleportation, non-demons who get teleport sickness might prefer that.

Speaking of... "Has anyone mentioned that you might feel a little sick after?" I give him a nudge to get him moving again. His neighbors are watching us, and I'm not sure how much his tools are worth, but I'm not in the mood to fight anyone off to protect them.

He makes a humming sound. "Maybe? I think I read something about it online. How does it work?"

I shrug. "Not everyone feels it, so you might be one of the lucky ones. But some people feel nauseous and dizzy—just like regular travel sickness. It usually passes fairly quickly." Unless he's one of the really unlucky ones who feels sick for hours. That's rare, though.

"I can handle that," he says confidently. "Are we going straight to the cave?"

Uh... "You don't want to see where you'll be staying and settle in first?" The town council wants to meet him, too, but not until tomorrow morning. It might be only midmorning here in Boston, but in Hortplatz it's already late afternoon, and everyone figured he'd want the evening to orient himself to the house we've got him in, maybe make a shopping list and walk around town. Sure, it's dark and cold and probably snowing again, if Zac's prediction was right, but it's February in Hortplatz, so that's what most days are like.

He shakes his head. "It has a bed, right? Or... somewhere to sleep?"

I look around for the person with the hidden camera, but there's nobody. "It has a bed," I confirm. "A very nice king-sized one with pillow-top mattress." The house is small, with only two bedrooms and a combined living-dining-kitchen area, but it's fresh and comfortable and only a block from the center of town. I designed it specifically for singles or couples without kids who wanted low-maintenance and proximity to action... such as it is in Hortplatz.

"That's all I need. I'll be spending all my awake time in the cave anyway."

I really hope he means that he sleeps for fourteen hours, because as the person who's been assigned to transport him back and forth and stay with him while he's there, I'm not prepared to sit in a cold cave for more than ten hours a day. I make a noncommittal noise. We can talk about this later. Maybe he'll get severely teleport sick, and we'll need to work out a different plan anyway.

"I guess we can go straight to the cave," I concede. "But only for a little while. I have some stuff to do tonight."

"Oh, you can just leave me there. I can make my own way back to the village. I assume it's signposted?"

It's my turn to stop dead, and when he doesn't notice, I reach out and snag his sleeve before he can take more than two steps. He turns around and blinks at me. "What? Was I about to trip?" Looking down, he turns in a full circle. "I don't see anything."

"Is this a test?" I ask, unable to resist. "Did someone pay you to do this?"

Cam frowns, and if he's not actually confused, he's a hell of a good actor. "No? I mean... am I getting paid for this? I don't remember if Alistair said."

I pounce on that. Alistair is my cousin Asher's husband's

cousin, and he's notorious for fuckery. This is definitely the kind of thing he'd do. "So Alistair put you up to this? It's fine —I can take a joke." I force a big smile, the kind even a non-demon would see. We demons have higher muscle density than other species—we need it to be able to teleport and stay healthy—and that means that our facial expressions are a lot more subtle than everyone else's. It's led to people thinking we're all grumps, since they can't always see when we're smiling or happy. As a result, most adult demons exaggerate things like smiles when we're around other species.

From the way Cam's eyes widen and he steps back, my smile might not have been the cheery kind.

"You have a lot of teeth," he whispers.

Okay. Toning it down. "Sorry. Uh... it's all good if Alistair's trying to prank me. You can tell him you got me. But—"

"Alistair's trying to prank you? How?" He looks around. "Is he here? I haven't seen him in forever." He frowns. "Or maybe it was last year? When did I make the puzzle that started out as a box but looked like a slice of cake when it was solved?"

How the fuck am I supposed to know that? Also, the puzzle that *what*? "We might be talking at cross-purposes," I admit. It's possible he's not pranking me. Or if he is, he's incredibly talented and deserves to see me make an idiot of myself. "Did Alistair ask you to play a joke on me? Or did anyone?" Because this is the kind of thing my cousins might do, too.

Cam shakes his head fiercely. "Not that I remember."

That's... weird. But I'm not going to ask. "Okay. Great. Then did anyone tell you exactly where we're going and what you'll be doing?" If he thinks he can walk along a signposted path from the cave to the village, he's about to get a serious shock.

"I'm solving the puzzle," he says promptly. "The stunning

puzzle door in the cave. Which is in Switzerland." His expression turns worried. "Don't you know where we're going?"

"I do," I assure him. "I think maybe you don't, though. What do you know about the village?"

"It's in the Swiss Alps, and the puzzle is there."

I'm sensing a theme here. Cam's focus is the puzzle, and hey, I can't blame him—it really is *awesome*. But I'm pretty sure Alistair or whoever else talked to him would have explained how cut off Hortplatz is during the winter, and it seems like he's so fixated on the puzzle that he just... didn't hear them.

I sigh. The middle of the sidewalk in a dodgy neighborhood isn't the place for me to explain everything, but I can't take him to the village or the cave without him knowing what he's in for. "Camden, I need you to listen to me." He winces slightly. Maybe because I used his full name after he told me not to, but I need his full attention right now. "Are you listening?"

"I'm not fucking five, you know," he retorts. "Of course I'm listening."

Taken slightly aback, I study him. I've been too preoccupied to really *see* him before now—first by the guy who might have been planning to rob him, then by Cam's apparent indifference to that, and after that it was just a blur of keys and bags and weird conversation. But now, I take him in properly.

And I like what I see. A lot.

He's shorter than me, but that's not uncommon—most demons are tall. I'd say he's probably about five eight? And he's lean. His hair is a tousled mess of dark blond curls, and his brown eyes seem to take up half his face. The other half is dominated by his puffy lips.

Those lips are right now sneering at me, and I don't hate it. He might be absentminded, but once he's paying attention, the attitude's there. I like feisty men, and he's got a lot for me to like.

Testing the waters, I smile slowly. My "wanna get hot and sweaty" smile. It took me a long time to perfect it, since it has to be visible to all species and make them want to tear my clothes off.

His mouth falls open and his eyes glaze over. "Hiiii."

It's never been that effective before. I clear my throat, a little uncomfortable... and turned on. It's too easy to imagine that mouth open for my cock. "So... Cam. It's not possible to walk from the cave to the village right now."

His expression clears a little, and he frowns. "It's not? Why?"

Okay, he seems to be hearing what I'm saying. That's a good sign.

"Because the village is high up in the Alps, and it snows a lot. The cave is even higher up, over an hour's walk on a clear day. There's a lot of snow right now, and while technically you *might* be able to walk it if the weather was good"—after all, my five-year-old brother did. That's how we found the cave— "it wouldn't be easy or safe."

His lip begins to tremble. "But... I need to get to the cave. I need to see the pretty."

I nod. "Yes, you do. That's why I'm here. My job is to take you to and from the cave every day and stay with you to help if you need it."

Cam shakes his head, already happier now that I've told him he can get to the cave. "I won't need help. I'm sure you have other things to do."

I do. I have six months' worth of client projects sched-uled, and the village council has been making noises about needing to expand if we want to attract other species to live in Hortplatz. As the architect who designed the current village, I'm the one they're looking at now. Sitting in a cold cave with no Wi-Fi is not conducive to getting all that work done. But there's no way I'd leave someone up there with no safe way to get back to the village and no way to contact anyone.

"The puzzle is my priority right now, and that means staying with you."

He frowns. "I could just call you when I need you to pick me up."

"There's no cell service in the cave."

Horror crosses his face. "Is there service in the village? And internet access? I need the internet!"

"The village has excellent coverage and internet," I assure him. We paid an arm and a leg for boosters or something that would give it to us. I don't know exactly how it works, only that Asher, who looks after the village's finances, bitched hard about the cost. It's worth it, though, otherwise we'd be even more cut off from the world.

He takes a deep, quivering breath, and it's so adorable I find myself leaning toward him.

# CHAPTER THREE

## Cam

He leans in, his handsome face intent, and I frantically check to make sure I'm not accidentally enthralling him. My control is good, but that happened to me once when I was younger, and I never want to do it again. Enthralling someone without their consent is gross.

But my powers are tightly under control, so that means he's—

Before I can finish the thought, he straightens, lips pressing tightly together. I'm not sure what made him change his mind, but I can't lie, I'm disappointed. It's been a long time since I fed the old-fashioned way with a good-looking demon who can probably handle me in all the right ways.

I sigh. Oh well. At least I'll have the pretty!

Which is apparently at the top of a snow-covered mountain. Alistair really should have told me that.

"Just to recap," I say, because this is important, "I can have daily access to the cave and there's internet and cell service?"

"In the village," he qualifies, his voice a bit rough. I pretend not to notice. "Not in the cave. But yes, I'll take you to the cave every day... though it would be fine if you wanted to take weekends off or something. I can even take you to Zurich for shopping or nightlife... or back here, if you want to spend the weekend at home."

Is he crazy? Why would I want time away from the puzzle?

Maybe he doesn't get it. I pull my phone out of my pocket and bring up the pictures Alistair sent me. "Here... look. This is what I'll be working on."

He glances at the screen, and his brow furrows in a frown before his eyes return to my face. "I know. I was one of the people who found it."

I grab his arm with both hands, dropping my phone. "You were? Tell me everything! Is it as amazing as the pictures make it look?"

For a second he just blinks at me, and I give his arm a little shake. A tiny smile appears on his lips. "It is," he admits. "Completely amazing. Incredible."

I sigh and sag against him. "I knew it would be. I can't wait."

"Let's get moving then," he suggests, bending to pick up my phone and handing it back to me. "I'll take you to the cave for a *very short* look, okay? Just a few minutes. No working, just looking. It's a lot later there, remember? And then we'll go back to the village and settle you into the house. Tomorrow morning, the village council wants to meet with you, and then I'll take you back to the cave."

I don't love the idea that my first visit with the pretty is going to be a short one, but I get it. I forgot about the time difference, and I guess it would be wrong to make him sit with me without giving him time to prepare first.

So I nod. "Sounds good." Except for the part about meeting the village council. "Why does the council want to meet me?"

He's looking over my shoulder, frowning fiercely, and I half turn. There's nothing there, just a bunch of teens who live on this street. "I'll tell you about it later," he says abruptly. "Let's not stand around here any longer."

I shrug. "Sure." The faster I get to the pretty, the better. "There's an alley just up ahead." It goes all the way through to the next block, but people hardly use it because... well, it's hard to pretend you don't see something when you have to squeeze past what you're trying not to see. I lead Micah toward it, then hesitate and peer carefully around the corner. I'm not really worried for myself—if I'm in danger, I can use enthrallment in self-defense. But I've heard that demons can be very extra when they feel attacked, and I don't want some hapless human ripped to literal pieces because he points a gun at Micah. So much easier to just roll his mind and make him think he drank too much and imagined us.

Thankfully, the alley is empty, and I pull him in, my suitcase dragging over the concrete.

"I guarantee you that people have died here," he says, his lip curling as he looks around. He's probably right, but since they're not here dying right now, does it matter?

"Is that important? Do you need the power of dead souls to help you teleport us?"

From the startled way he looks at me, I'm guessing not.

He shakes his head and holds out a hand. "Come here."

I put my hand in his, and he pulls me to his side and wraps an arm around me. "Ready?"

I'm too busy enjoying the sensation of his muscles pressed against me to understand what that question really means. "Yes," I say, wondering if he'd notice if I turned and plastered my front to him. Maybe wrap my arms around his wais—

The world spins, the alley blurring into gray nothing and then into... blackness.

"Whoa." There's solid ground under my feet, but I can't see...

Light spears out, and I blink and look away as it sears my retinas. Micah lets me go and steps away, and I realize the light is the flashlight on his cell phone.

"Let me just turn on the lights," he's saying, and in a flash, I realize what this means.

We're in the cave. The puzzle is almost within arm's reach!

I make myself stand still. The last thing I want is to accidentally trip on something and hurt myself when I'm *this close* to the pretty. I can be patient, even if it does feel like I'm actually vibrating from the excitement.

Lights flash on, and I squint. It looks like they have some portable work lights set up, similar to the ones used for night-work on the roads or construction sites. That'll be handy, since one thing I forgot about caves is that they're dark.

But the lights aren't what I'm here to see, and I turn around, looking for the—

There it is.

Wow.

I head toward it, my gaze crawling over every inch. The photos told me it would be spectacular, and oh, it really is.

A hand clamps down on my shoulder, preventing me from getting to the pretty, and I whine and squirm.

"Easy," Micah says. "You were about to walk into the crate."

I blink and glance down, and sure enough, there's a wooden crate right in front of my left leg. That would have hurt.

"Thank you," I say over my shoulder to Micah, but he doesn't let go.

"Just a quick look, remember?" he prompts. "And how are

you feeling after your first teleport? Any queasiness, headache?"

Frowning, I tear my attention away from the puzzle door and turn toward him. "Nothing like that. I feel fine." I try to remember the seconds after we teleported, when it was still dark. Did I feel ill then? "I don't think it affected me at all."

"That's great news. It's going to make all of this so much easier." He sounds relieved. I guess it might have been uncomfortable for me if teleporting made me feel sick but I had to do it twice a day to get here. "Anyway... this is it. The crates have all the components that we think are needed. They're numbered, and we think that's supposed to be the order of use. But I can show you that tomorrow."

"Tomorrow," I affirm, dodging around the crate and making for the wall. Door. Whatever. I need a good look at it before he makes me leave, and I suspect that's going to happen soon.

Up close, even in the not-ideal lighting, the puzzle is... perfect. I can't think of another word. It's huge, of course, but even on a small scale, it would be perfection. The intricacy, the *joy* of it... My eye tracks the patterns, looking for the starting point, but then an anomaly leaps out at me. Oh ho. The designer of this liked tricks, it seems.

This is going to be so much fun.

I finally let myself reach out and touch. The metal is cold under my fingers, slightly pitted with rust in places. Not badly enough that it's going to be a problem, but still. It's a crime that this wasn't taken better care of. Sure, being in a cave in the middle of nowhere would make maintenance harder, but I'm here, aren't I? As long as people can get here, there's no excuse.

"You should be ashamed," I chide, and footsteps come up behind me.

"Why?" Micah asks, suddenly a lot closer than I thought he'd be. I resolutely keep my focus on the wall.

"Look at the state this is in. Why hasn't someone been cleaning it, or at least set up a dehumidifier in here?"

He makes a sound I can't interpret, and I take my hand off the wall and turn to look at him. His face gives me no clues—demons are so damn hard to read. They either want to murder you, or they feel nothing. I'm never sure which it is.

"Well? Nothing to say in your defense?"

"In my defense," he begins drily, "we had no idea this was even here until two weeks ago, when Isaac, my five-year-old brother, decided to go for a walk and find the cave an imaginary dragon was living in."

I blink. "There's a dragon living here?" It's a nice enough cave, as caves go, but not exactly luxurious. Or even comfortable.

He shakes his head, and this time I'm pretty sure his dark eyes are amused. "No. Isaac heard a story—a made-up story—about a dragon who lived in a cave on a snowy mountain, and because he's five, he figured it might be true."

That sinks in, and I shudder. "But you said it's over an hour walk through the snow to get to the village from here."

"We were all very panicked at the time. Fortunately, we found him—in this cave. Which we didn't know existed before then. Our village has only been here for the last fifty-two years, and the area was mostly abandoned before that."

I look around the cave again, and finally spot what might be the entrance. It's more of a crack than an opening, barely wide enough for an adult to squeeze through, and the only reason I see it is because a small flurry of snow happens to blow in at precisely the right moment. Now that I'm paying attention, the wind is howling a bit out there.

But... "This isn't enough rust damage for fifty years. Someone must have been looking after it."

He pinches the bridge of his nose. "It's a really long story. Why don't I take you to the village and tell you over a meal? Are you hungry? It's nearly dinnertime."

I think about it. I skipped breakfast because I was so excited, and it's been hours since then, so I guess I should eat. "I forgot to throw out the leftovers in the fridge," I remember. Oh well. Truthfully, they were leftover from like two weeks ago and were already too funky to eat. I'll just clean the fridge out properly when I go home.

Micah looks a little confused. "Do you want to go and do that now?"

Aw, he's sweet. I reach up and pat his cheek. The light bristle of his five o'clock shadow against my hand is... nice. Tingly nice. "Nah, that's fine. I guess I should have dinner, though. Is there somewhere we can go? I'm not the best cook. Plus I have no groceries. Do I? Does my place even have a kitchen?"

He's starting to look like he regrets ever inviting me to eat with him. "The pub serves dinner. There's a diner and a coffee shop that are open during the day, but they close at four. Your house has a *great* kitchen"—he puts a weird emphasis on "great," and I wonder if he has a kitchen fetish— "and we stocked it with basic groceries, but there's no need for you to cook tonight. If you don't feel like going out, I can cook. Or we can eat with my cousins. They'd love to meet you."

I scrunch up my face. "The five-year-old?"

He chuckles—an actual baby laugh. It suits him. "No, Isaac will be home with our parents. My older cousins were also part of the group who discovered this cave. And Garrett —do you know him? He's Alistair's cousin."

I relax. "I don't know him, but if he's related to Alistair, we're already friends." Any friend of Alistair's is a friend of mine.

Micah shakes his head. "Sure. Of course. Come on, let's get back to the village. We'll sort out dinner there."

I cast one last longing glance at my pretty. Tomorrow, I'll get to play with it.

## CHAPTER FOUR

### Micah

Impatiently, I listen to the phone ring. He better damn well pick u—

"Did you get him? Garrett's about to burst a blood vessel here." Asher doesn't bother with anything as mundane as a greeting. I can't believe he manages to negotiate multimillion-dollar agreements with those social graces.

"Hello to you too," I snark. "I'm fine, thanks."

"Why wouldn't you be fine? I saw you just a couple hours ago. Did you go get Camden?"

I give up. "Cam," I correct. "He prefers to be called that."

"He prefers to be called Cam," Asher relays to Garrett. Why he doesn't just put the phone on speaker, I have no idea.

"He's checking his tools," I continue, then stifle a snort. That came out way dirtier than it was meant to. "The work tools he brought with him," I clarify, but Ash doesn't even seem to have noticed. He's always been overly responsible and kind of boring. "What are you guys having for dinner? Is there room for us?"

"Zac's cooking. I think he said something about chunky soup and cheese toasties?"

My mouth waters. Zac's nowhere near a gourmet cook, but his chunky beef and vegetable soup is always good. "I'll check with Cam, but if I don't call you back, we'll be there in about twenty minutes." He shouldn't need more than that to check his tools (haha), right?

Maybe I can offer to check them for him.

I hang up on whatever Asher's saying to give that intriguing idea some more thought. There's no denying how attracted I am to Cam. If we hadn't been standing in the middle of a street, likely to be mugged any second, at a time when I was supposed to be bringing him here, I would have kissed him before. My common sense might have won that battle, but even my common sense thinks he's sexy and wants to spend some fun time with incubus dick.

The thing is... I'm not sure if he's attracted to me too. I *think* he is, but incubi are known to be flirty. They feed off sexual energy, and an intense flirtation can be a nice snack for them. Or so I've heard. I'm still not completely clear on how it works. Whatever, I don't want to assume that he's into me and make a move that might make him feel uncomfortable because he was just being himself. I need a sign.

"Hey, Micah, is there anywhere in town I can buy some toothbrushes?" He bounces into the open-plan living area where I'm standing, almost but not quite bashing his shoulder against the doorframe.

"Uh, yeah. The supermarket has them. It's closed now, but I'm sure I have a spare at home if you forgot to pack yours."

He waves that off. "Oh no, it's in case I need them to clean off the rust. I have one in my kit, but that's a big wall."

Can't argue with that. "I was just talking to my cousin Asher." I change the subject. "He's the one who's married to Alistair's cousin, Garrett. Did you want to eat with them tonight? My other cousin, Zac, is cooking beef stew."

His already glowy face lights up. "Homemade stew? That sounds *divine*. Will there be crusty bread too?"

"Cheese toasties, Asher said."

He frowns for a second. "Oh, you mean grilled cheese. That's even better than crusty bread. Cheese makes everything better."

I leap on that opportunity. "If you like cheese, some of the best cheesemakers in the world are in this region. Maybe one day we can go and see them, get some samples." I try not to cringe. *Get some samples?* I'm not usually this bad at life.

To my shock, he's nodding enthusiastically. "That would be awesome. But not until I've had some time to play with the puzzle. I'm not ready to leave it yet."

"Of course." I try not to sound awkward, but I'm busy trying to work out if this means he likes me, or he likes cheese. Could it be both?

"Do your cousins live far from here?" he asks next. "I know you demons like to teleport everywhere, but is it walkable? It looks like the snow might be easing up."

I glance out the window. It's hard to tell with the lights on inside, but it does seem as though it's barely snowing right now. If the snowplow went through earlier and Zoe, our snow management sorcerer, has done her rounds this afternoon, it should be clear enough to walk. The snow's not slushy right now anyway.

"We can walk," I agree. "It's only a few houses down this street. But you'll need to bundle up." The cave was cold, but still sheltered. I don't think he realizes how cold it's going to be outside. The wind isn't that strong down here in the village, but there's still a definite wind chill factor in play.

"I can bundle up," he promises. "What a coincidence that your cousins are so close!"

Not much is really all that far in a town of a thousand

people, but yeah, it is a coincidence that this house was empty right when we needed somewhere to put Cam. "I live there too," I tell him, trying not to think about how convenient the location is. Not that I couldn't just teleport here if I wanted to, but being so close means that he can come over easily as well. Especially now that we're making an effort to keep the streets clear for our non-demon residents, of which, including Cam, we have five. It might not seem like a lot, but six months ago we had zero, so we're definitely making progress.

"You live with your cousins?" He frowns. "Didn't you say one of them is married?" I open my mouth to explain, and his eyes go wide. "Ohhhhhh. Don't worry, I don't judge. As long as everyone's happy and everyone consented, I'm good with anything."

It takes me a second to process that and realize what conclusion he's come to, and then I laugh so hard, I think one of my organs might have ruptured. My knees give way, and I sink down onto the two-seater sofa and clutch my sides in an attempt to stop the ache.

When I can finally breathe again, I swipe the tears from my eyes and sigh. He's watching me with a grin. "You have a nice laugh. You should use it more often."

"Thank you. Uh, about my cousins—"

He holds up a hand. "Nope. I got it. Not a poly and minorly incestuous relationship." He pauses. "Is it incest when you're cousins?"

Shrugging, I say, "I've never needed to know. But cousins can legally marry in most countries, so maybe not? Or it's not legal incest, even if it is... something." I can't imagine wanting to hook up with one of my cousins. They're like brothers to me.

Although I hear some people are into that too.

"When the town was being built, we decided to share a

house so families could get their own houses faster," I explain. "And then that was working for us, so we just never bothered to change. But now that Asher's married, he and Garrett will move out—they're waiting for the thaw to build their house. Asher's had the plans for about forty years, and Garrett only wanted minor changes made." That's probably more information than he needs, but the architect in me finds it essential.

"And then it will just be you and your other cousin? What was his name again?"

"Zac. Yeah, it'll be just us. Zac's easy to live with, especially in summer, when he's out camping half the time. He's the unofficial ranger for the town."

Cam comes to sit beside me, his eyes bright. "Why unofficial?"

Huh. "I don't know," I admit. "Probably because the village council never got around to creating the job. Zac just kind of stepped into the role, and he's been doing it ever since." I should talk to him about that. The least the village could do is pay him a stipend—not that he needs it, with Asher looking after his money, but fair is fair.

"What do you do, when you're not babysitting me? No, actually, *why* did you get stuck with me?" He folds his arms across his chest and frowns. "Not that I'm not grateful for your help, but sitting in a gloomy, cold cave all day isn't going to be fun for you. I hope they're paying you well."

I make a mental note to talk to the village council about their habit of co-opting me and my cousins for jobs and then not paying us. Because I'm pretty sure nobody considered giving me money when Grandmother volunteered me for this role. They definitely didn't pay me for designing the village, all those years ago. "Your questions are connected," I tell him. "I'm an architect, and I used to be an engineer... still am, technically, since I keep up my accreditations, but I don't practice anymore. That incredible feat of engineering in the cave is right up my alley, so to speak, and the council"—my grandmother—"thought I might be able to help you, since I have some understanding of the engineering of it. Plus, this way I get to watch you solve it."

He's smiling widely. "Watch me? Nah, you can help! Do you like mechanical puzzles?"

"I haven't had a lot of experience with them. The good ones are hard to get hold of, especially out here, and I'm too much of a workaholic to go in search of them." I try not to wince as I basically tell him the thing he spends his life creating isn't important enough for me to spend time on.

He either doesn't notice or doesn't care. "This will be a real treat for you, then. You're starting with the emperor of puzzles!" Even if I wasn't already excited for this, I would be now. His enthusiasm is contagious.

My phone beeps, and I glance at it. "Dinner's going to be ready in a few minutes," I warn. "Go grab your gear if you want to walk." I don't have mine with me, since I'd planned to teleport from warm room to warm room, but demons have higher muscle mass than other species, and I'll be fine for the less-than-five minutes we'll be outside.

Cam scrambles to his feet and beelines for the doorway. His shoulder bumps it on the way through, and I wince. That will probably leave a bruise.

He's back a minute later, pulling on a wool peacoat, and I make a mental note to get him some proper gear. That's not going to keep him warm. I glance down at his running shoes, which are definitely not going to hold up to the snow. "Do you have boots?"

He blinks at me. "Not the kind I'd wear in the snow. And I didn't bring them with me anyway."

I don't bother to remind him that I can go pick them up. If they're not appropriate for the sn— What kind of boots does he mean?

Pushing aside the image of something thigh-high in shiny leather and maybe with a heel that would make his legs look a million miles long, I stand. "Okay. We'll get you something tomorrow. We're not going far tonight anyway." I gesture to the door. "Dinner awaits."

# CHAPTER FIVE



## Cam

Micah wasn't wrong when he said I'd need to bundle up. It's *freezing* outside. Also, there's more snow than I expected. The road has at least a few inches, and the front yards of most of the houses are drifted high. Is that what the road looks like when nobody's cleared it? It's possible I wasn't prepared for this. Sure, Swiss Alps means snow, but the picture I had in my head doesn't match up with snowbanks four feet deep. Or this bone-aching cold. I'm going to need to layer up a bit more if I ever want to leave my house. And get boots, because the cold is seeping through my running shoes.

Micah glances back at me, his hands shoved deep in his pockets, and grins. "We'll get you a warmer coat," he promises. I don't know if he can read my mind or what, but I'll happily go along with that plan. He's not wearing a coat at all, just the jeans and sweater he had on before, and I wonder how he's not frozen solid.

He turns into the front yard of a two-story house. Unlike most of the others on this street, the front path is neatly shoveled, allowing easy access to the front door. I guess that makes sense, if Alistair's cousin lives here. A hellhound wouldn't be able to teleport in and out like the demons can.

I eagerly follow him inside, shuddering in the amazing warmth. "That was *brutal*," I gasp. "I thought I liked snow, but I was wrong."

"Thank you!" a voice exclaims, and I turn to see a shifter in the doorway to what seems to be the living room. This must be Garrett. He's got a less intense vibe than most hellhounds, who tend to vibrate with leashed energy. I get a more laid-back, professorish signal from him. "I keep telling everyone this is not the nice kind of snow, but they just laugh at me." He smiles and comes forward with his hand outstretched. "I'm Garrett Smythe."

"Alistair's cousin." I take a step, trip, and end up diving at him. Luckily, Micah moves fast and catches me before I can knock his cousin's husband to the ground. That's not the kind of first impression I want to make. "Whoops. Sorry."

Garrett's still smiling as Micah stands me upright. "Are you okay? Did you trip over..." His words drift away as his gaze drops to my feet. "Oh no, your feet must be soaked! Get out of those shoes and I'll get you some socks to wear. Frostbite is a real concern up here, you know."

"He doesn't have frostbite," Micah scoffs. "He was barely out there long enough to get wet feet. He just needs to dry off... and let me buy him some boots."

I sniff, because I *could* have frostbite for all he knows. My feet certainly feel cold enough. Although isn't lack of feeling one of the first signs of frostbite? Okay, I probably don't have it, but he can't just go around assuming he knows things, even when he does.

Garrett gives Micah a look that makes me like him a lot, then goes to find the promised socks. Focusing on my feet, I see what concerned him so much—my running shoes are clearly soaked through. I toe them off—the undone shoelaces were what I tripped on, though I could have sworn I tied them before leaving the house—then bend to peel off my socks. A hand lands on my shoulder, steadying me.

"Thanks," I say—a little grudgingly, because he didn't *know* I was going to fall over. Just because it might have happened doesn't mean it was going to.

"You're welcome. What size shoe do you wear?"

I blink as I straighten. "How should I know?"

"They're your shoes," he points out. "When you buy them, what size do you get?"

"Whichever one fits." He can't be that dense, right? I mean, why would I buy shoes that don't fit?

Sighing, he bends over and snags one of my running shoes, then looks at the inside of the tongue. "Ten," he mutters. "Are these comfortable for you?"

"I wouldn't wear them if they weren't," I assure him. He seems to have a weird relationship with shoes.

Garrett comes back then, followed by another tall demon who looks enough like Micah that I assume it's one of his cousins. "Here you go." Garrett passes me a pair of thick wool socks. "Put those on and warm up. I'll stick your socks in the dryer and put your shoes on the radiator." He stops short and frowns at Micah. "Why are you holding Cam's shoe?"

"I'm checking the size." Micah holds the shoe out to Garrett. "But I'm done."

Garrett looks like he wants to say something but decides against it. Instead, he sweeps up my other shoe. "This is my husband, Asher, by the way," he says instead. "Ash, meet Cam Torrence."

Oops. I never ended up introducing myself properly to Garrett. Lucky he already knows who I am, but I need to do better. People are always saying I get distracted too easily. "Hi," I chirp with a little wave.

Asher's stern face softens a little and he shoots a glance at his cousin. He's not quite as handsome as Micah, but there's something very dependable about him, and when he transfers his gaze to his husband, it's so full of love, I almost "aww" out loud.

And then that love changes to something else, and my energy levels get a little ping. Note to self: If I'm not getting enough sexual energy, spend some time with Garrett and Asher. If a single glance boosted me, a kiss could probably feed me for a week.

"It's nice to meet you," Asher says. "We're very grateful you were able to make time for us."

I laugh, then realize laughing in his face isn't polite. "I'm grateful to *you*," I explain quickly. "That puzzle is *stupendous*." I wave my hands for emphasis, notice that I'm still holding the socks, and sit down on the floor to put them on. When I scramble to my feet again—this time with them encased in lovely warm wool—Garrett and Asher are both smiling at me. Asher's smile is barely there, but I can still see it.

"I really hope you like it here," he tells me. "Come and meet Zac."

I trail after Garrett, through a living room and into an eat-in kitchen, with Micah and Asher following, murmuring to each other. My hearing is good, but not quite good enough to catch what they're saying. Garrett must, though, because at one point he looks back at them and clears his throat loudly.

In the kitchen, another demon is stirring a pot on the stove while grilled cheese sizzles in a pan. It smells wonderful in here, and my stomach growls loudly. "Oops," I say sheepishly as all eyes turn to me. "I skipped breakfast."

"We'll get you fed," the new demon assures me. "I'm Zac. Excuse me for not shaking your hand, but we're at a critical point."

"No problem," I say.

"A critical point of stirring soup?" Micah scoffs. "You're making that up."

Zac turns back to the stove. "Do you want to interrupt me and risk ruining dinner?"

Micah huffs and rolls his eyes but doesn't say anything else, and I hide a smile. That's so cute. Like an oversized know-it-all kid. If he pulls that shit with me in the cave, I'll make him stand outside.

"Can I get you a drink, Cam?" Garrett asks, and I realize I haven't had anything to drink since my wake-up coffee. I'm parched.

"Yes, please," I say gratefully.

"I can get it," Micah volunteers. "We have beer and wine, sparkling water, soda... and juice boxes."

"Juice boxes?" I bite my lip to keep from giggling. "None of you seem like the juice box type."

"My brother and Asher's sister like to visit sometimes. The juice is for them, but they'd be happy to share."

They keep supplies for their siblings? That's sweet. "Thanks, but soda is fine."

"Sit down and be comfortable," he... orders. His intent is nice, even if the delivery is lacking. I glance over the round kitchen table, which is set for dinner.

"Anywhere in particular?" I ask. I don't want to sit in someone's preferred seat. I hate when that happens.

Garrett smiles at me knowingly. "Right there is a good spot. And it's next to me."

Thankful that he's making it easy for me, I slide into the seat he indicated.

"Dinner's ready," Zac declares, sliding the last grilled cheese sandwich onto a platter and bringing it to the table. "Ash, help me dish up."

Asher goes over to the stove with a stack of bowls as Micah delivers my soda and takes the seat beside me. "Okay?"

he asks quietly, and I can't help my little grin. People always say demons are grumpy, and I avoided them a lot because of that, but these guys are great.

"Okay," I affirm and take a sip of soda.

Zac and Asher join us a moment later, passing out the food, and for a little while, there's just the sound of eating with the occasional "mmm" of pleasure. Zac makes excellent soup. If I was the kind of person who cooked at all, I'd ask for the recipe.

"So, Cam," Garret says, finally breaking the silence. "How do you know Alistair? I was surprised when he said he knew a mechanical puzzle expert. He's not the type to sit down with a puzzle."

I snort. "No," I agree. "They're not energetic enough for him. It's a good story, actually. I was working in a department store in... hmm. I think it was the 1960s? A good while ago, anyway. I hated it, but it was steady work, and I needed the money. They stuck me in the back of menswear, because sometimes I can be clumsy, and they figured that's where I'd do the least harm." I roll my eyes. That was a stupid assumption—in the two months I worked there, I did a *lot* of accidental damage. "The plus side to being in such a quiet corner was that nobody noticed if I kept a puzzle with me and fiddled with it when there were no customers."

"I can't relate any of this to your cousin," Asher tells Garrett. "A quiet menswear department? There's not enough chaos for him there."

This time I laugh out loud. "He brings the chaos with him. One day, the store was practically deserted, and I was playing with this puzzle I'd made myself. It wasn't quite what I wanted it to be, and I was just wondering if adding components would make it better, when I heard shouting and a massive crash. People were yelling, and this man comes racing through the store, being chased by another man. The first guy was knocking over displays and weaving, doing his best to avoid being caught, and I was getting annoyed. I was the one who'd have to clean that mess up, you know?"

Zac winces. "People suck."

I nod. "They really do. Anyway, he came charging past me, and I threw my puzzle at him. It hit him in the back of the head and knocked him out."

"Please tell me that was Alistair," Asher says. "Please."

Garrett elbows him. "He's my cousin, Ash. It looks terrible for us to hope he got injured." He turns his gaze to me. "But was it?"

I shake my head. I'd be appalled by their callousness, but... it's Alistair. He's a wonderful friend to me and a lot of fun at parties, but I don't think anyone who knows him hasn't wanted to maim him a little at least once. "No, Alistair was the one chasing him. I never found out exactly why, though—he said it was classified. He put handcuffs on the guy, handed him over to a bunch of officers from Enforcement who'd finally arrived, and then brought me back my puzzle, thanked me for helping, and asked me what it was." I pause to take a sip of soda, and everyone waits.

"Did he listen to your answer?" Garrett asks.

"He did." And now that I know him better, I marvel over that. Alistair can be focused when he's interested in something, but mechanical puzzles don't interest him. "He even asked questions. And then he invited me to a party he was throwing that weekend."

Garrett nods. "Yeah, that sounds more like Alistair. So you were friends after that?"

"Yes. It's kind of impossible to not be friends with Alistair if he wants you to." I don't go into any detail about everything Alistair's done for me. I barely know these people, and even though they've been so nice to me, they don't need to know my deepest, darkest secrets.

# CHAPTER SIX

## Micah

I guess I should be glad Alistair didn't want to be friends with me. I don't think I could handle his kind of friendship—Garrett's more my kind of hellhound. But there's something about the way Cam's face changes when he talks about being friends with Alistair that makes me wonder if there's more to the story. Maybe they hooked up for a while? I'm sure if they'd been in an actual relationship, Garrett would have heard about it. Hell, the way Alistair shares things, he probably would have told us when he first mentioned Cam.

Whatever. I might be interested in Cam, but even if we do hook up, that doesn't give me any rights to his past, and I wouldn't want them anyway. We're grown adults, not jealous adolescents.

"Did you have a good trip?" Garrett asks, changing the subject. "I hope the teleport sickness wasn't too bad." He makes a sympathetic face. It still hits him every time, even though he's used to being teleported now. At least it's not too severe.

"Oh, I didn't get sick," Cam says blithely and bites into

the toastie he just dunked in his soup. Garrett's eyes flash to me.

"He didn't," I confirm. At first I'd thought he may have been playing it off, and of course I couldn't tell in those initial dark minutes in the cave, but I paid close attention when I brought him to the house. He's either a helluva actor, or he really doesn't get teleport sick at all.

"That's great." Zac sounds surprised, and he grins at Cam. "It's going to make teleporting back and forth from the cave so much easier."

Garrett nods. "I'm jealous," he confesses. "I still get queasy every time. Not bad enough to throw up, but it's not fun."

"Wow, really?" Cam's eyes widen. "I had no idea. It didn't feel like anything to me. I mean, when it was dark in the cave, that was a bit disorienting, but I didn't feel sick."

Asher raises a brow at me. "You've been to the cave already?"

"He was excited to see the door." That's kind of under-stating it.

"I was going to die if I didn't see it today," he confirms in a matter-of-fact tone that makes me wonder if he would, indeed, have died. Even though I know he wouldn't have. "And I'm so glad Micah took me. It's stupendous!"

Garrett's grinning widely. "Isn't it? I never could have imagined something like it."

"But I was surprised by the amount of rust," Cam contin-ues. "Micah said it's been fifty years since anyone's been there, but there's not enough rust for that."

"That's not what I said," I correct before either of my cousins can make a smart-ass comment. "I said the village has been here for fifty years and we didn't know the cave existed."

"But someone else must have known and been looking after it," he insists stubbornly.

"Wait," Zac interjects. "Alistair didn't tell you the background?"

Cam shrugs. "He might have. I was looking at the pictures."

Asher turns slowly to look at me, and I shrug too. The horror on my cousin's face is kind of fun.

"That's okay," Garrett's saying. "That means I get to tell you, and it's a fun story." He repeats what I told Cam earlier about Isaac wandering off and us searching for him. "And then he didn't want to leave because he hadn't had a chance to look at the 'treasure,'" he continues. "And in the middle of telling him there is no treasure, we actually looked around and saw the wall and all the crates with the components in them."

"Wow," Cam breathes. "That must have been incredible."

"It *was*. We had to go home, though, and come back the next day with equipment because Zac's a party pooper."

"Hey! While you slept in, I was running around getting all the stuff we needed," Zac protests. Garrett ignores him.

"Then we had to call the government—or in this case, Alistair and these guys' cousin, Gideon. They brought their experts, and it turns out the whole thing is actually the door to a dragon hoard that's been there for thousands of years."

Cam's jaw drops. "But... but there's not enough rust for that!"

Garrett nods slowly. "Right? The dragon who created it used some really good preservation spells. We had two dragons here looking at them saying how good they were."

"Wowwww," Cam breathes, and I choke down the impulse to lean over and kiss his cheek. "This is... this is..." He shakes his head. "This is so much better than I thought it was, and I already thought it was going to be the best part of my life, ever."

"There are better things coming your way," I advise him. I

don't know why. I just feel like he deserves all the best things, and a cold, dark cave is not the pinnacle of his life.

Well, maybe his professional life.

He looks at me like I'm insane. "That's sweet, Micah, but there's nothing better than this. A twenty-foot complex mechanical puzzle designed by a dragon and forgotten for thousands of years? It's like a dream come true."

"Yeah, Micah," Asher goads. "It's a dream come true." He smirks at me. Dammit, he's guessed that I'm attracted to Cam. Not that it would be unusual—Cam's very attractive. But I was hoping my cousins wouldn't notice.

"It's a dream come true for me too," Garrett says in a quelling tone, glaring at his husband, and it's my turn to smirk at Asher. "I'm a social anthropologist," he explains to Cam. "Just thinking about what we can learn from whatever's behind that door..." He gives a little shiver. "The dragon wing leader said he doesn't think it's a personal hoard, so I have high hopes that it's some kind of archive."

"A magically preserved archive from all those years ago?" Cam lets out a low whistle. "It really is treasure."

Garrett seems thrilled to have someone to geek out with, and he pushes his empty bowl away and leans forward. "Right? And we've been promised that a dragon will come and help us go through the contents. We'll probably need some community historians too, but I'm excited to talk to a dragon. Talk properly, I mean, and ask them questions. The kids are excited too."

Cam blinks. "You have kids? Are they in bed already?" He turns to frown at me. "You should have said so I could bring them puzzles."

My brows pull together as I try to work out how I'm at fault for not telling him about the kids Garrett doesn't have. On the plus side, he's not pulling away from me even though I'm frowning. I like that.

"Oh no, we don't have kids," Garrett says, clearing things up. "I meant the village children. I'm running the school this year, and they're all very excited about the idea of meeting a dragon." He hesitates just a little, and Zac snickers. We all know that Garrett has plans for Cam to meet the kids and talk about puzzles... he just hasn't told Cam that yet.

"Actually, I was wondering... would you be interested in speaking to the kids? They've heard about the door now, of course, and they're all fascinated by the idea of a giant puzzle with moving parts."

Cam lights up. "Sure! Maybe they could do a field trip to the cave and see it for themselves?"

"No," Zac says immediately. "Sorry. You'd need too many adults to teleport them in, and the cave isn't big enough."

Cam squints one eye closed. "Really? It seemed pretty big."

"There's seventy children at that school. Right, Garrett?"

"Seventy-four," Garrett corrects, looking crushed.

"That means more than thirty adults to teleport them, and over a hundred people in the cave at one time. With all those crates..." He shakes his head. "I'm really sorry, but I just don't think it would be safe."

"What if they do it in shifts?" I suggest impulsively. Cam's downcast expression is spurring a hitherto unknown fixer instinct in me. "Different groups on different days."

Cam and Garrett both turn hopeful eyes to Zac, who sighs. "Maybe. Put together a plan and I'll think about it. But Cam, won't that many sessions interfere with your work?"

"Yes." Cam nods solemnly. "But this is important. Mechanical puzzles teach fine motor skills, spatial reasoning and logic, and also allow processing time for people suffering from PTSD and other mental health challenges. These kinds of puzzles made a huge difference to my life when I was a kid, and I think all children should be introduced to them." He turns to Garrett. "If the kids can't come to the cave, I'll come to the school and show them some cool puzzles."

Garrett smiles gratefully at him. "Thank you. That's so kind. If there's anything you need while you're here, please call me. I'll give you my number. And you should eat with us whenever you like."

"I like to eat." Cam nods emphatically. "I'm not a good cook, though. Or any kind of cook."

"What do you do for food?" Asher asks.

Cam shrugs. "Takeout. Sometimes I get those instant meal things from the grocery store, the ones you just have to heat up? But if I've forgotten to shop, they don't just magically appear in my house." He seems put out by that.

"Definitely eat with us," I say. It's not like he's going to have many other options, if he doesn't cook. The pub is the only place open at dinnertime, and they don't deliver, so on a bad night, he'd have to slog through the snow to get there.

Which reminds me... I clear my throat. "On the topic of food... well, sustenance... Alistair mentioned that since you'll be spending so much time in the cave, away from the village, it might be necessary to take extra steps to keep you sustained."

Cam gazes at me blankly. "Extra steps?"

I feel my face getting hot as I remember what Alistair actually said, which was that I should wank in the cave. "Uh, he meant... you're an incubus." Hopefully that will make everything clear.

"Yes. I'm aware."

Okay, so maybe not. I shoot Garrett a pleading look. He has more experience dealing with other species socially than I do.

Garrett smiles at the tabletop and says nothing. This is probably his revenge for the time I accidentally told Isaac that hellhounds shit glitter. Meanwhile, Cam's still gazing enquiringly at me.

"Well, I don't know a lot about it, but incubi need sexual energy to stay healthy, right?"

"Yeah," he agrees. "Oh, I get it now. Because I'll be spending so much of my time in the cave, it cuts the number of hours I'll be able to feed. Hmm. I hadn't thought about that."

It's become apparent to me, in the few hours I've known him, that unless it's directly related to puzzles there are a lot of things Cam doesn't pay attention to.

"How many people are in this place, again? Like, sexually active adults. And how spread out are they?"

"Around nine hundred," I tell him. "The village covers an area of just over a square kilometer." As the person who designed the village, those facts are burned into my brain.

"What's that in miles? I'm American, and we don't cope well with the metric system."

"A bit more than half a mile."

He screws up his face like he's thinking. "And there's no negative feelings toward sex, right? Like... a chastity cult or something?"

Zac coughs, and I fight against the laugh that wants to explode from my chest. He's being serious, and this is an important subject.

I can't quite manage an answer, though.

"Nope!" Garrett announces cheerfully. "The village has the same healthy attitude toward sex that the rest of the community does. If you want it, have it. If you don't, don't. No human religious puritanicalism here!"

"Is that even a word?" Asher asks him, and he shrugs.

"It is now. Language evolves over time, and I'm evolving it."

Cam doesn't seem to notice the byplay. "That's good. That

many sexual people in that area should generate enough passive energy to keep me going." He frowns. "Oh, but I'll be in the cave for a lot of the day."

Asher shoots him an incredulous look. I get it—we were talking about the cave, so how could he have forgotten the cave? But I'm accepting the fact that Cam's priorities are different from ours, and that means his brain works differently. Or maybe it's the other way around.

"Hmm. If I start getting lethargic and spacey, you might need to take me to a more populated area," he instructs me, and panic stabs my chest. He already seems a little spacey to me—does that mean I need to act now?

"What would that look like?" Garrett finally steps in to save me. "I've never been around an incubus or succubus with starvation sickness."

"I've had it so many times," Cam announces cheerfully, as though his life wasn't at risk. "I get caught up in work and forget about everything else, sometimes. It's easier to order takeout food than it is to order a takeout sex worker."

# CHAPTER SEVEN

## Cam

In the middle of taking a sip from his glass, Zac snorts soda up his nose and makes a sound somewhere between a yell and a squeal. "That burns! Fuck!"

Asher passes him a napkin and then turns his intense gaze on me. "A takeout sex worker? Is that a thing?"

I glance around the table. Garrett's the only one who doesn't seem fazed. Micah's staring with his mouth open and a glazed expression. It's cute. I like when the big, tough-looking guys get all flustered. "Not as much of a thing as I wish it was," I reply. "Last-minute requests for a sex worker to come to your home—someone you know has consented to the work, not been trafficked or forced into it by circum-stances—are expensive, and while my puzzles sell well, they don't sell that well."

"So what do you do?" Zac asks, fascinated.

I shrug. "I bought a house that's close to strip clubs. There's enough residual lust to keep me fed. Before that, I used to have to leave my house and go in search of a hookup or something."

Micah looks confused. "I'm sorry, I don't mean to be insensitive, but how does it work, exactly? I know you don't have to have sex, but is watching a stripper enough?"

I sit up straighter, enjoying this. Most people already know this stuff. I never realized I'd enjoy educating others on the needs of my species. "That's not a yes or no question. A stripper is doing their job, right? So there's no guarantee they'll be turned on as they perform. Maybe they will because they like being watched, or maybe they're thinking about their grocery list. If I'm the only one there, watching them, my own arousal won't feed me."

"Ahh." He nods. "But in a strip club, there are other people watching and getting turned on."

"Exactly."

"But you can use enthrallment to feed, can't you?" Zac asks. "Doesn't it cause arousal?"

I try not to be offended. He's asking because he doesn't know. Maybe it's weird that he doesn't know, but still, he's trying to learn. "I'd only do that if I was genuinely starving and had no other options. Taking away someone's right to consent is gross."

He shudders. "I hadn't thought of that. I liked it—when I was with an incubus who enthralled me, I mean. But he asked me beforehand if I was okay with it. I might have felt different otherwise."

I smile at him. "Yeah. Even if you're consensually having sex with someone, enthrallment is something that needs to be discussed." I glance around the table. "Is it okay if I ask... You all seem kind of sheltered?"

Garrett starts to laugh, and I grin. I like him. He's not as bold as Alistair, but also not as annoying. I think he and I could be friends... as long as I don't get too caught up in work and neglect the friendship like I usually do.

That's one thing about Alistair I can't complain about. He doesn't care if I forget he exists. He just cheerfully pops up in my life and reminds me.

"Yes," Micah says. "I'll explain in a minute. Can we just go back to feeding you for a second? I don't want to fuck this up."

Aww. That's sweet. "It wouldn't be you fucking up," I point out. "It would be me. And I've done it heaps of times, so I'm not worried."

"I am," he counters. "We don't have dial-a-sex-worker in Hortplatz, *or* a strip club. Is it safe to teleport you if you have starvation sickness?"

I shrug. How should I know? "I can't see why not."

He doesn't look reassured. "And when you say 'lethargic and spacey,' does that mean I should be on the lookout for yawning? If I call your name and you don't respond immediately, do I need to step in?"

"Depends. If you call my name and I don't respond while we're having dinner, and I'm also not really eating or paying attention to anything, then yeah, probably. But if I'm working on the puzzle, try calling a couple more times. I might just be concentrating."

His frown gets deeper. "And what do I do? Take you to a strip club? Or should I find a reputable escort agency that will send someone on request?" He turns to Asher. "Your apartment in Zurich would probably be the best place."

"Why don't you just do what Alistair suggested?" Zac says slyly. "Once or twice a day, and you won't need to worry about any of this."

Micah's face flushes dark pink. "Shut up," he mutters, glaring at his cousin. It's the cutest thing, and I prop my chin on my hand and enjoy the sight.

"What did Alistair suggest?" I ask.

The table falls silent, and all eyes turn to Zac. Who also blushes. "I think he was probably joking."

"Great! I like to laugh." I know I'm being a dick now, but these demons are kind of fun to torment. I never knew demons were so adorable. They spend all that time being glowery and grumpy, but turns out, they're teddy bears.

Zac looks like he wants to be anywhere but here, and Micah's buried his face in his hands. I was only teasing before, but now I really want to know. "He—uh. He said that Micah should... you know. While you guys are in the cave."

Ah. I actually do know, because this is a joke Alistair has made before. From anyone else, having a houseguest offer to "watch porn and wank in the guest bedroom if you need me to" would be creepy and disturbing, but somehow, he makes it not weird.

I'm not sure how.

Regardless, I'm having too much fun to say anything other than, "He should what?" and blink innocently.

Micah gives an agonized moan, and Zac swallows hard. "Uh... masturbate." He says the word so fast, it's almost unintelligible.

"Ohhhhh." I nod. "Sure. That would help."

Micah whips his head up. "What?"

The horror on his face is too much for me, and I start to laugh. By the time I've got it under control enough to speak, they're all in on the joke.

"That was mean," Zac chides, but he's grinning. "I nearly sweat blood."

"Sorry, but it was too much fun to pass up." I flick a glance at Micah, whose face is no longer nearly purple. "For the record, any enjoyable sexual activity—like masturbation —would help to feed me, but I definitely don't expect you to get your cock out in a cave. I'll be fine. If you're worried, you can check in with me regularly about whether I need to feed."

"Wow," Garrett says. He seems to have enjoyed the past few minutes as much as I have. "You mean Micah doesn't have to go all control freak? He could just *ask* you how you're feeling?"

"I'm not a control freak," Micah argues. "You're confusing me with your husband."

Garrett snorts. "Please. All three of you—and Gideon, too—are control freaks. You get it from Damaris." He winces and looks around.

I look around too, but I don't know what we're looking for.

"She can't hear you," Asher says dryly. "She's three blocks away."

"With her, you never know," Garrett whispers.

"Who's Damaris?" And do I want to meet her or avoid her? It's hard to tell.

Micah smirks. "Our grandmother. You'll meet her tomorrow. She's on the village council."

"You'll be fine," Garrett reassures me, even though I don't know why I need to be reassured. "She's happy about the cave."

"Now," Asher mutters. I feel like there's a story there, but I want to get back to my earlier question before we start shooting off on tangents.

"You were going to tell me why nobody knows much about incubi," I remind them. "Also, now that I think of it, do you not have *any* living here? That's... weird." I know the place gets cut off by snow, but it still seems weird that nobody from my species lives here.

"One of my teachers at the school is a succubus," Garrett volunteers. "But other than her—and she's only here until June—no."

"Really? None?"

Micah sighs. "Aside from Garrett and his staff at the

school, and Zoe, the sorcerer who clears out the snow, there are only demons living here."

I process that. "Is this payback for me teasing you before? You're trying to trick me now?"

"It's not that weird," Asher protests. "It just... happened that way."

"It's weird," Garrett tells him firmly, then turns to me. "What I've been given to understand is that demons originally liked to choose settlements based on how defendable they were."

"That sounds sensible." I have no idea if it is or not, but defending a settlement has to be a good thing, right?

"It is. But the most defendable places are the ones that can't be accessed easily. For demons, that's not a problem—they can teleport. But a lot of others don't want to live somewhere that's so hard to come and go from."

I nod, getting it. "So it ended up being just demons living there."

"Yep. When they moved here, to Switzerland, it was the same story—they picked this place because it's away from human eyes and they don't have to hide as much. But it's cut off by snow for a quarter of the year—"

"What?" I lean forward. "Cut off? Like... nobody can leave? At all? For *three months?*"

"It's not that bad," Zac murmurs.

Garrett glares at him. "Not for you, who can teleport anywhere you like anytime you like."

Micah leans in and whispers, "Garrett's still mad because we forgot he'd be trapped in his house after the first blizzard."

I turn to look at him and find his face only inches away. A tingly shiver shoots through me, the kind I haven't felt in too long. The downside of passive feeding via nearby strip clubs is that I haven't bothered to leave my house and have sex anytime recently. I wonder if Micah would be willing to end my dry streak.

"Why was he trapped?" I whisper back while Garrett and Zac bicker.

Micah shrugs. "We didn't have a snowplow then. Or Zoe."

It dawns on me what he means, that the snow was so deep, Garrett literally couldn't leave the house. No wonder the whole village gets cut off.

It sounds perfect. No outside world to bother me, just uninterrupted time with my puzzles. Too bad there's also no takeout delivery. Starvation would ruin puzzle time pretty quickly. No wonder there are only demons living here.

"But you have the plow now?" I check. The road was definitely plowed when we walked over here, but still... I don't love the idea of starving to death. Or what if I run out of a number four bolt and need to run to the hardware store? I can't do that if there's snowdrifts taller than me at my front door.

"And Zoe," Micah assures me. I'm still not entirely sure who Zoe is, but she seems to be part of the snow removal process, so that's good.

"And there's really only a handful of non-demons living here?" Even knowing the circumstances, that seems incredible to me. I may not be the most social person in the world, but there's comfort to be taken from being part of the community of species. I can't feed from another member of my own species; not really. Knowing there are others who know what I am and will consent to me feeding from them without me having to endanger myself... that's priceless.

"Yep," Garrett says, overhearing and breaking off his argument with Zac, which seemed to have morphed into an exchange of "No, you're the worst!" He squares his shoulders. "That's part of the reason why I'm here: to help the village think of ways to attract other species. And whatever's behind that door in the cave is going to be a big part of it."

I take a second to think about that. Historic treasure hidden by a dragon thousands of years ago behind a door that's a puzzle? Definitely sounds like a tourist attraction to me. And where tourists go, others follow to cater to them.

"Good thing I'm here to open it."

# CHAPTER EIGHT

## Micah

If Cam hadn't been so adamant earlier about the importance of consent, I might wonder if he was enthralling me. Because all I can think about right now is getting my hands into those blond curls and my mouth on his.

To be closely followed by my mouth on other things.

Sitting next to him at dinner might have been a mistake, because the scent of him has been in my nostrils for hours: machine oil and Dove soap. Not the sexiest combo, but it's driving me wild.

"...at least it's breakfast, and we'll send food with Micah for lunch," Garrett's saying as he hands Cam a cotton tote bag of food. I zoned out while he was packing it, but given Cam's declaration that he can't cook, I really hope it's stuff he can eat as is.

"Thank you. I'll hit the store... sometime. I guess tomorrow. Before we go to the cave, maybe." He doesn't sound too excited, probably because that means less time in the cave.

"Between this and what we already stocked in the kitchen, you should be okay for a few days," Garrett assures him. The two of them seem to have already formed a bond, and I'm glad. It didn't take long to guess that Cam would easily spend all his free time alone with his puzzles. He needs more friends like Garrett.

And me. I can be his friend. It's okay to lust after friends, right?

I don't get the chance to decide for sure, because Cam turns his big brown eyes on me and says, "Okay, I'm ready. You can take me now."

*Oh, baby.*

He means take him back to his house, of course. Not... take him. Even though he's only going two houses down, I'm teleporting him there. It's too cold outside, and he's not dressed for it. Garrett solved that problem, thankfully—he and Cam put their heads together over his phone and did some online shopping. His new coat and boots will be ready for collection at a store in Zurich tomorrow. Asher's going to get them, since he has to go for a meeting anyway.

Until then, I'll teleport Cam wherever he needs to go, and make sure he's wearing warm layers. The last thing we need is for our puzzle expert to get sick. Grandmother wouldn't be pleased.

Just the thought of my grandmother (and her frown) is enough to kill off any lingering inappropriate thoughts I might be having. "Let's go," I tell Cam, trying to sound casual. "I'll be back in a bit," I tell my cousins. Zac's wandered off somewhere, and Asher's frowning at his phone, but Garrett smirks.

"No rush," he says. Why did Asher marry him, again?

I put my hand on Cam's shoulder and take us both to the teleport room in his house. There's nothing special about it— it's just a small room that's kept empty to make teleporting into it safer. Like all teleport rooms, there's a poster on the wall with a unique identifier—something to fixate on and teleport to. In this case, it's a photo of the front of the house with the street name and number underneath. All I had to do to get here was picture that poster.

Much better than slogging through the snow and wind.

Keeping my hand on Cam's shoulder so he doesn't get disoriented, I reach out and flip the light switch. When I said the room was small, I meant it. We purpose-built this town, and I designed all the houses to have a teleport room. There was no point in making them big rooms; most are the size of a closet.

"Thank you," he says politely, blinking in the sudden light.

"My pleasure." I take my hand off him, already regretting the need to stop touching him. "I'll leave you be. You've got my number if you need anything?" I check. We did the whole exchange numbers thing before.

"Sure, but..." He looks up at me, and I swear, I could drown in those eyes. "Why don't you stay?"

"Stay?" I repeat, not sure what he means. Does he need my help with something? "And talk about our plans for tomorrow?"

He shrugs. "We could do that, if you want. I was hoping we could have sex."

I stare at him. "Sex?" Is this... Am I dreaming?

His gaze turns to concern. "You have had sex before, right? I didn't get the impression that you were celibate."

"No—I mean, yes. I've had sex. I'm not... celibate."

He smiles brightly. "Oh, good. I can tell you want me, but that doesn't always mean a person wants to act on it, you know? And you totally don't have to. But if you're up for it, sex would be nice."

Sex would be... nice.

It takes a second for my brain to fully process what's on offer. "Yes! Sex would be nice. We can have sex. If you're sure you want to," I add, my conscience nagging me. "Please don't be concerned about not being fed or anything. We can make sure you get enough sexual energ—"

His laugh cuts me off. "Trust me, Micah, if I didn't want to fuck you, I wouldn't be offering."

Finally, I manage to pull myself together. "Then yes, I absolutely want to have sex with you."

"Great! Come on. This room isn't going to suit what I have in mind." He grabs my hand and leads the way into the hall, then unerringly to the master bedroom. He flips the light switch, and I gasp.

"You've been robbed!" His stuff is strewn from one side of the room to the other; on the bed, the floor, the dresser. There's even a sock hanging from the curtain rod. "Stay here while I make sure they're not still here." I can hardly make myself believe it—we have such a low crime rate here. Who would break into the house of a man who came here to *help* us? It's not like he's going to have a lot of stuff worth stealing —he's only visiting.

"I've been robbed?" He grabs my arm. "No, don't go— what if they hurt you? Call for help first. Let's lock the door." Pulling me the rest of the way into the room, he closes the door and snibs the lock. It's not going to stop anyone who wants to get in, but it'll give us warning, at least. I stride over to the en suite bathroom and make sure the thief isn't hiding in there.

"Okay," I declare, pulling out my phone as Cam goes through his things. He seems most worried about the tools laid out on the dresser. "I'll call my cousins, and we'll make sure the house is secure. Did they take anything valuable?"

He shakes his head. "I don't think they've taken anything at all. There was a TV in the other room, wasn't there? Maybe they got that." He starts toward the door, as though he's going to check, and asks over his shoulder, "How did you know I'd been robbed, anyway?"

Uh-oh.

I look around the room again. Could this be the way he left it? "Hold up a second." He stops and turns toward me. "I'm not sure how to say this without sounding like a judgmental asshole."

"A judgmental asshole?" He seems confused, and then a grin spreads across his face. "Ohhh. A judgmental asshole. Yes, Micah. I'm a messy person. Don't tell me: you're a neat freak."

I wince. "Not exactly. But... the sock, for example?" I point to the curtain rod.

He glances up. "Oh yeah. It was in my way."

The sock was in his way. And somehow that led to it being thrown onto the curtain rod.

I nod, because I don't know what else to do. "I'm not familiar with that method of sock storage," I say, sounding like an idiot.

He laughs, and the sound thrills through me, making my dick chub up in my jeans. "Just to be clear," he starts, "if I tell you this mess was made by me, that means nobody broke in and we can start getting our clothes off?" His gaze meets mine, amused and direct and full of promises.

My mouth goes dry. "Yes."

"Excellent." He sidles closer and lays a hand on my chest.

"Very excellent." I don't know what else to say. My cock is straining against denim. Thinking is beyond me right now.

"Before we get naked and sweaty," he says, his tone suddenly serious, "we need to talk about what sex with an incubus is like."

I blink a few times and then realize what he means. "You mean enthrallment?"

He nods. "We don't have to do that. It's not necessary for me to have and enjoy sex."

That's good to know, but... "What if I want to?"

His grin flashes before he hides it behind his serious face again. "Then we can. A light enthrallment won't completely take away your ability to think for yourself. It will ramp up the sexual connection and make things... hazier." He hesitates. "You need to be very sure you want to do this, because once you've been enthralled, your decision-making will be impaired."

He looks up at me earnestly, and I want to take hold of him and never let go. His concern for my consent is heart-warming.

"I trust you not to do anything that would cross my boundaries," I tell him. "I want to do this with you. As far as what happens... just ordinary sex this time—no experimenting or kink."

Cam nods. "I think you should top this first time." He pauses. "Uh... you do top, right? I like to switch."

"I top," I assure him. In fact, I've only ever topped. Does this mean he might want me to bottom in future? I'm not sure how I feel about that.

My uncertainty must show on my face, because he says, "Are you sure? Beca—"

"No, I'm sure. I top."

He gets it then. "Oh. I like bottoming, Micah. It's fine if you don't want to switch."

That's good. Right? Except now that the thought is in my head, I think maybe I shouldn't be so quick to dismiss it. "Let's focus on tonight."

His smile returns. "So... we're good to go?"

"Very good. Me topping, vanilla sex, enthrallment included. Yes?"

His answering "Yes" has barely left his mouth before his fingers are tearing at the buttons of my shirt. We get naked as fast as possible, falling to the bed in a tangle of arms and hands and mouths—

"Ow!" I pull back from Cam's kisses to toss aside the shoe I landed on.

"Okay?" he murmurs, licking down the side of my neck. I don't bother to answer—I'm busy exploring the narrow expanse of his chest. The blond curls on his head are repeated there, finer and paler, but just as pretty, and I thread my fingers through them, grazing over his nipple in the process. His tiny growl is music to my ears.

I work my way down his body, ignoring his protest as I move out of reach of his mouth. He can have his turn to explore later. His dick is standing at attention, and I wrap my hand around it. I've never seen an incubus cock up close before, and it's fascinating. I knew what it would look like, of course, but that's not the same as holding it and feeling the shape for myself. The "waist," nipped in like a wasp's body, is even more defined than I thought it would be. I think about how that would feel entering me, and suddenly I'm even more curious about bottoming than I was before.

But now's not the time to think about that. I bend my head and lick the tip of his dick. He makes a sound of encouragement. "I want to be your all-day sucker."

Uh. What?

I lift my head to stare at him, and he shrugs. "I guess I'm not that good at dirty talk."

"The premise is good." I pat his thigh reassuringly, liking the idea of sucking on his cock all day long.

"Oh, good." He hands me a packet of lube. "Take care of this, will you? And then you can fuck me until my ass reshapes itself to fit only you."

My head spins with the thought, precum leaking copiously from my cock. I tear open the packet and make quick work of prepping him—not that he needs much. His muscles relax almost the second I touch him, letting my fingers slide in and out of his hole with little resistance.

"Mmm." His eyes slide closed. "Love this."

My breathing speeds up, gaze locked on his flushed face and blissful expression. "I can tell."

Opening his eyes, he looks directly at me. "I want more."

I withdraw my fingers, and he adjusts his position on the bed. The puckered pink skin of his entrance beckons me, and I line my dick up, pressing forward against the fluttering resistance of the muscle.

"Micah?" Cam's voice draws my attention to his face. "Are you ready?"

My cock throbs in response. "I've never been so ready for anything."

In the next moment, a fog of lust sweeps over my brain. I *hunger* for Cam, for his body, his ass. My hips surge forward without conscious thought, desperation to take him seizing every atom of me, and as my thick, hard dick drives into him, it drives into *me*. We cry out in unison, and I realize that I'm feeling what he is. Panting, I thrust, dying to conquer, to send him insane with the same wild desire and pleasure I'm drowning in. Each movement, every breath is an echo, a dizzying double-hit of sensation, his and mine, of quivering, tightening muscles and sparking nerve endings.

Higher and higher, tighter and tighter, more and more, Cam's excitement and need flooding my brain and pushing me faster until his orgasm floods through me, swamping me with pleasure and making me come so hard, the world fades around me.

# CHAPTER NINE

## Cam

"Cam? Come on, it's time to wake up," a familiar deep voice coaxes. A hand lands on my shoulder, not quite shaking, but definitely not letting me sink back into the glorious arms of sleep. "Cam?"

I groan, haul the covers over my head, and snuggle down. Micah might be an excellent fuck and a nice guy, but I'm not waking up.

Micah.

The puzzle!

My eyes snap open, but it's dark under the duvet. I sit up and slam my head into something hard that yelps. Fighting with the duvet that really doesn't want to let me go, I call, "Micah? Help!"

He mutters something, then that hand is back, holding me still, and he peels the duvet off my head. I inhale deeply and blink up at him.

"That wasn't what I imagined when I pictured dying in bed."

He stares at me, face set in frowning lines. I'd be worried that he's angry, but I only have to remember what his face looked like last night, and how affectionate and cuddly he was after, to banish any concerns. He might seem scary, but he's a softie.

"You pictured dying in bed?" he asks.

I shrug and crawl off the mattress, nearly taking a header over the edge. Fortunately, he catches me. I rise on tiptoe and kiss his cheek. "Thanks! And yeah, every incubus dreams of dying in bed. Just not in our sleep." I wink, then saunter toward the en suite bathroom. "Just let me use the facilities and then we can go to the cave."

His voice follows me. "Use the facilities and then I'll take you to meet the village council."

Shit, I forgot about that. I spare a longing thought for my pretty puzzle, all alone in that cave, as I flip up the toilet lid and take care of business. Why do I have to meet the village council, anyway?

I shout the question to Micah and hear him sigh.

"Because they want to meet you. It won't take long, and Garrett will be there."

He will? I flush and wash my hands. "How is he on the council if he only came to live here last year?" Should I shower? Probably. Micah and I were enthusiastic last night, and there's cum crusted in all sorts of places. Demons can't smell as well as shifters, but they smell well enough that they'll know what we were up to if I don't shower.

"He's not on the council," Micah calls patiently through the half-closed door as I turn on the water. "They appointed him to be the point person for anything to do with the cave, though, so he's coming to the meeting this morning."

It seems like every time I learn something new about the situation here, I end up with thirty more questions. None of them matter, though, except "But then we can go to the cave?"

He chuckles softly, and the sound of it makes me smile as

I open the cabinet under the sink and find a big, soft bath towel. "Yes, then we can go to the cave. Unless you want a tour of the village or to go to the grocery store."

"I can do that on the weekend when you make me take time off." I'm only half joking. Now that I know Micah has to be with me while I'm in the cave, I don't feel as opposed to taking weekends off. It's not fair to make him give up all his free time. Especially because I'm almost positive he still needs to work at his day job. Which is... engineering. No, architecture! He used to be an engineer, and that's why he recognizes how amazing my puzzle is.

I stick a hand under the water and find it's reached a delightful temperature. "Do you want to join me in here?" I call as I step under the spray. The shower itself is perfection —big enough for three people, with a rainwater head and jets on the sides. If metal didn't rust, thus making it impossible to bring puzzles in with me, I'd move into this shower.

Micah appears in the doorway, and I peer at him through the steamy glass. "We don't have time for me to join you," he says, but his eyes are hot as they skim downward. I'm not sure how much he can see with the steam playing peekaboo, but I slide my hand down my stomach to my cock anyway. The way his breath catches tells me he gets the idea.

"Are you sure? I can be fast."

His nostrils flare, and for a second I think I have him. Then he takes a step back. "You have no idea how hard it is to say no to you right now."

I pout and turn back to the spray, hopefully giving him a great view of my ass. "Then why did you?"

"Because I don't want to tell the council the reason we're late is that we fucked in the shower. Ten minutes." He leaves before I can reply.

I reach for the shower gel. Any other time, I might pout and take extra long, but why punish myself? I want to get to the cave, and that means meeting with the council. How bad can it be?

ℳ

I'm reminded of that question twenty minutes later when we step out of the teleport room at what Micah tells me is the post office and see Garrett with an anxious face.

"Thank fuck. I thought you were going to be late."

Micah looks at his watch. "We've got three minutes still."

"Yes, but she's—" Garrett cuts himself off and widens his eyes.

"What?" Micah groans. "No. Why?"

I look between them like a spectator at a tennis match and wonder if either of them will finish a sentence that's longer than one word. Context would be helpful here.

Before I can ask, Micah sucks in a deep breath and turns to me. "Be polite. Answer their questions. Don't say anything... Don't say anything else. Do *not* tell them I took you to the cave yesterday or that we slept together. Don—"

"You slept together?" Garrett whispers, but it somehow seems almost as loud as a yell.

Micah shoots him a flat look. "You knew that. Remember me coming home this morning and you making a smart-ass comment about me being in my clothes from last night?"

"Yes, but..." He stops and shrugs. "I have nothing. I knew, but I didn't want it to seem like we'd gossiped about it." He turns to me. "We didn't."

I shrug. "I don't mind if you did. Just as long as you're all saying nice things." Not that there's anything else they could say. I was in that bed with Micah. He had no complaints. "But why are we suddenly afraid of the council?"

"We're not afraid," they protest at the same time, then exchange embarrassed glances. I roll my eyes and cross my arms, propping my shoulder against the doorframe we just came through. Somehow I miss and plunge through the doorway, headed for a painful sprawl on the floor.

Micah's hand closes around my upper arm with an iron grip and hauls me upward. He waits until I'm steady on my feet before letting go. "Okay?"

I peek up at him coquettishly. "My hero."

Garrett chokes back a laugh, but Micah's breath hitches even as his cheeks flush. Someone else might have thought that was embarrassment, but I'm an incubus. I know what turned-all-the-fucking-way-on looks like. So Micah likes the idea of being my hero? I file that away for future reference. Role-play sex is fun.

I'm just wondering how to convince him to sneak into the bathroom for a quick blowjob—is there a bathroom here? There must be—when Garrett yelps. "We're late!"

Micah seizes my hand and drags me along the hall. Thankfully, we don't have far to go, because my coordination isn't great even when I'm not unbalanced and racing with no clue where to go. We pause for a moment outside the door to catch our breath, and then Garrett opens it and steps inside.

I follow right on his heels. They never explained what the big deal was, and now I'm eager to see this council that can fluster them both so much.

At first glance, I don't get it. There are seven demons sitting at a boardroom-style table. Some of them look older, even for our lifespan, and none of them seem particularly young. That's probably normal, right? People with experience get elected or selected for village councils.

"There you are," a woman snaps. If I had to guess, I'd say she's the oldest one here, but she doesn't look elderly. The way she's glowering does make me want to take a step back, though.

Fuck that.

"Sorry we're late," I announce cheerfully, stepping around Garrett and taking a seat at the table. It might look ballsy, but mostly it's so they can't see my knees knock together. "My fault, I'm afraid. I'm clumsy, and Micah had to save me from falling over."

There's a moment of silence as they all try to work through that, and Garrett and Micah join me at the table.

"Are you hurt?" the dark-haired man at the head of the table asks at last.

"Only my pride." I pause. "And definitely my dignity."

The man's face relaxes in a way that makes me think he might be smiling... but not. "Those are easier to heal than broken bones. I'm Jesse Hatt, the demon species leader. Welcome to Hortplatz."

"It's nice to meet you." Shit. Why didn't Micah mention the species leader of all demons was going to be here? I wouldn't have waffled on like an idiot. "I'm Cam Torrence, and I'm here to solve the pretty. I mean, the puzzle. The door." Dammit, they know that. Time to zip it. I should have listened to Micah when he said not to say anything.

A warm hand lands on my thigh under the table and squeezes lightly. I let out a little breath. Micah's got my back.

Jesse introduces the other council members. When he gets to the scary older woman, Damaris Bailey, something clicks in my head. This is the grandmother everyone was talking about at dinner last night. The one they reassured me was happy about the cave, as though it would be a bad thing if she wasn't.

Looking at her now, the frown on her face sending genuine shivers down my spine, I get it. No wonder Micah was willing to give up shower sex with me. I wouldn't want to piss this woman off either.

She doesn't say hello, or acknowledge me in any way, really, unless you count the slight intensification of her glare.

I'm just wondering if Micah's reflexes would be good enough to teleport me to safety *before* she lunges at me across the table, when Jesse asks, "Could you tell us how you plan to work?"

Tearing my gaze away from Damaris, even though every prey instinct in me insists I should keep my eyes on her, I blink at him. "Um. Sure. Micah will teleport me there and back each day. But not on weekends, because he deserves time off. Especially if he has to keep doing his regular job as well."

Beside me, Micah shifts uncomfortably, and I realize I've made it sound like he's been complaining to me. "He's been so helpful and welcoming," I add, and Garrett makes a tiny sound on the other side of me. Oh yeah, I guess in the context of us having fucked all night, that might be a weird thing to say. But the council doesn't know that... do they?

I glance around the table. Nobody's smirking or shocked. They don't know.

"We never doubted he would be," Jesse assures me. "Micah has always done his duty well and faithfully."

I frown, because that definitely didn't sound right, but he's still talking.

"I actually meant, what's the process for solving the puzzle?"

Oh.

# CHAPTER TEN
## Micah


As Cam smiles sheepishly at the council, I try to sneak a glance at Grandmother without her catching me. I still don't know what has her on the warpath this morning, but she's not in a good mood. She's been positive about the impact the cave could have on the village, so I'm pretty sure that's not it. I'd know if someone in the family was sick—I spoke to my mother this morning.

Whatever's pissed her off, I hope it's not something I did.

"The process is simple," Cam's saying. "Whoever designed this wanted people to be able to open it."

"That's highly doubtful," Grandmother scoffs. "If they wanted it to be opened, why would they make the key so difficult?"

"Fun," Cam corrects, and there's this moment of suspended horror from the rest of us. People don't just *correct* Grandmother. Not when she's in this kind of mood. But Cam doesn't seem to notice. "The puzzle needs to be solved, sure, but all the components are there, in numbered groups. If they didn't want the door opened, they could have jumbled everything together randomly, or even not had them there at all.

Then you'd need to work out what pieces were required and source them. Some of those components are definitely not available mass-produced these days, so you'd need to commission a blacksmith or a factory to make them to spec... which you'd need to calculate and draw." He smiles. "That would have been fun."

Grandmother glares. Cam's eyes widen a little, and he inches his chair closer to mine.

"Since the components are all there," Jesse interrupts, getting things back on track, "how will you approach things?"

"Well, with the crates all numbered, there are only five possible options for the first component, which is great. The trick will be finding the starting point on the door. I was looking last night, and while there are several patterns that seem obvious at first, they're false leads."

"You went to the cave last night?" Grandmother asks sharply, and I try not to hold my breath. There's no reason why Cam shouldn't have gone to the cave last night, officially, but Grandmother's been around for a long time and prefers some of the old-fashioned formalities—like meeting the town council before any other steps are taken.

"I have pictures," Cam says smoothly. "Alistair sent them to me when he told me about the project. I hope that's okay?"

It seems I've underestimated him—not a word of a lie was told, and yet the danger has passed.

"So how will you find the starting point?" Jesse seems quite desperate to keep this from devolving into an argument —or worse. He's an excellent species leader, but Grandmother doesn't make it easy for him.

"Trial and error, probably. I'll keep looking for patterns, but it's most likely I'll find it by accident. Once I have it, it'll be easier to pick out the pattern I need to follow and start solving."

Mayim, one of the younger members of the council, leans

forward. "So the hard part is finding the first step? And once you have that, because the components are in numbered boxes, it will be easy? Anyone could do it?"

I look at the table so nobody can see my wince. What a great thing to say to a subject matter expert.

"Anyone could do it now," Cam counters. "It would probably take them longer to work it out if they don't have as much experience as me, but you don't need special training to solve a puzzle."

My wince turns to a smile. I should have known that when it comes to anything puzzle related, he'd be able to hold his own.

"I think Cam's being modest," Garrett interjects. "Micah, you're an engineer. What are your thoughts?"

Wow, he's still getting revenge for that whole "poops glitter" thing. Definitely never getting on his bad side again. "I agree; he's being modest. I've spent some time studying that wall and still haven't found the starting point. But even if I had, and even with the numbered crates, there are dozens of options to consider for each step. Yes, eventually anyone could solve it, but without an understanding of mechanical puzzles and a lot of experience, it could take years."

"*Years?*" Grandmother stands and plants her hands on the table. "You're exaggerating."

I shake my head. "No. The first crate has five possible components that can be attached to each element on the door. We don't know which element is the first one that needs to be solved. Those door elements also move in several directions. They have to be in the right position with the right component attached. I didn't check all the ways they could be positioned, but my guess is about twenty possible combinations for each element. And then—" I glance over at Cam, who's watching me with a soft smile. It's nice. "Correct me if I'm wrong, but without knowing the exact sequence, each time you complete an element, you'll need to check all the ones surrounding it to find which is the next one?"

Cam nods. "Yep. Once the pattern's established, it will go faster, but for the first twenty to fifty elements, I'll be working without direction."

"So you're looking at about a hundred and sixty or so possible options with each step... once you've found the starting point," I conclude, and Grandmother sinks back into her seat.

"I see," she murmurs. "And do you still think it can be completed within a few months, Camden?"

"Cam," he says instantly. "Sure I do. I'm not very good at keeping the fridge stocked or cleaning the house, but I'm excellent with puzzles. The first week will go slowly, but after that, the pace should pick up. I'll keep you informed, anyway."

She nods. "Then we'll leave it in your capable hands. We apologize if we implied your skills weren't extraordinary." She side-eyes Mayim, who shrinks back in her chair.

Cam cocks his head. "I like you," he tells Grandmother, and I tense. "You're scary as fuck, but not everyone will admit they might have been wrong."

Garrett's wild-eyed gaze meets mine, and I know what he's thinking. If I grab Cam and teleport, can we escape Grandmother's wrath?

She stares at him, and then her gaze swings slowly to me. Is she... is she going to hold me responsible for what he says? No. She might have a short temper, but she's always been a reasonable woman.

Mostly.

Sometimes.

She looks back at Cam and says, "Thank you. I like you too. Micah will bring you to our family dinner this weekend."

I will? I mean, I was going to ask if he wanted to come

anyway, since he's here alone and the only people he knows will all be there, but this sounds suspiciously like an order.

"He doesn't have to do that," Cam announces. "Though a plate of leftovers would be nice."

I stand. "We should get to the cave and start work. Lots to do!"

"Bring him on Sunday," my grandmother orders. There's no mistaking it for an invitation this time.

"Of course," I promise. Cam opens his mouth, possibly to argue, and I squeeze his shoulder. She seems less angry now, and I don't want to change that.

He gets the hint and aims a sunny smile around the table. "So nice to meet you all!"

I hustle him toward the door, Garrett on our heels.

"Garrett, stay," Grandmother says, and I don't look back. She likes him, so he'll be fine.

Once we're safely in the hallway, I slow a little.

"That was your grandmother, right?" Cam asks. "She's epic. But I wouldn't want to be trapped in a dark alley with her."

I slow a little more. "Why would you be trapped in a dark alley at all?"

He shrugs. "There could be reasons."

I leave it alone. I don't want to know what those reasons are, anyway. "Yes, that was my grandmother. And you're coming to dinner on Sunday, or I'll be in trouble."

"Are you sure I won't be intruding? Because I can stay home. Food is good, though."

"You won't be intruding." I stop walking. I don't know where I was even going anyway, since we'll be teleporting out of here. We need to go back to my place and grab the winter gear Garrett's lending him. The cave is sheltered and comparatively warmer than outside, but still too cold for him to be in there all day in just that peacoat. Tonight, Asher will bring the stuff that got ordered online. "Grandmother invited you. That's the opposite of intruding. And the food will be good. She likes to cook, and so does my uncle." Asher's dad makes the best roast potatoes I've ever had, and I'm a potato afficionado. "Are you ready?"

He looks up at me with those big eyes I just want to fall into, and says, "Sure. Ready for what?"

I have a strong suspicion that's how he approaches most things in life: first the yes, then the questions. "To teleport."

"Oh! Sure, let's go."

Garrett's left the stuff piled on the couch, and I leave Cam to put it on while I go and get my own gear. Plus my tablet. There's no internet connection in the cave, but I can do some design work if the opportunity arises.

When I get back to the living room, Cam's wearing the down parka and boots—which are definitely big for him, so I make a mental note to keep an eye out for extra clumsiness—but not the rest.

"You need those too," I say, nodding to the gloves, hat, and scarf on the couch.

He shakes his head stubbornly. "They'll annoy me."

I can see how the gloves might, since he'll be working with his hands, but that's all the more reason he needs the hat and scarf. I fold my arms over my chest and stare him down.

He stares right back.

The stare-off goes on for several minutes. Neither of us is willing to budge.

Finally, Cam grins. "You're so adorable with your 'I'm a scary demon, you must bend to my will' glare."

I falter. What?

He steps close and rises on tiptoe to kiss my cheek. "I'll wear the hat, but not the rest. They'll get in my way. And tonight, you can check every inch of me for frostbite."

Heat floods through me at the thought, but... "If you feel

any numbness or tingling, let me know immediately. Okay?" Frostbite isn't a joking matter.

He rolls his eyes. "Sure."

"I mean it, Cam. *Immediately.*" I'm going to have to ask him every hour. Wait... how long does it take for frostbite to take hold? I wish I'd listened to Zac when he was lecturing us about this. I just figured either I'd be able to teleport out of the cold, or I'd be so injured or weak that frostbite would be the least of my concerns.

"I promise," he says, seriously this time. "Now can we go?"

"Hat."

With a cute little huff, he turns toward the couch and trips over the too-big boots. I knew that was coming. Once I have him steady on his feet again, he grabs the hat and jams it on his head. "Happy?"

I examine him from head to toe. Garrett's nearly five inches taller than him and more solid, so Cam looks like he's playing dress-up. I wonder if I can take a picture.

"Okay, let's go."

He takes hold of the suitcase with all his tools. I jam his gloves in my pocket—just in case. Then I wrap my arm around his shoulders and take us to the cave.

# CHAPTER ELEVEN

## Cam

The moment we arrive in the cave, even though it's dark, I sigh happily. I can *feel* the pretty waiting for me. Micah goes to put the lights on, and I wait, not at all patiently. Honestly, if it wasn't for all the crates spread out through the cave and these damn boots that don't fit, I would have tried groping my way toward the wall. But that would be asking for a broken leg, and I don't have time for anything that might interfere with me solving this puzzle.

The lights flash on, making me squint, and I walk carefully, lifting my feet properly with every step. I still manage to misjudge one of the crates and bash my hip against it, but that's a minor inconvenience. Incidentally, the wall is *not* in the direction I thought it was when it was dark, so just as well I stayed still.

Micah joins me, and we both stare up at it. "Well?" he asks. "How can I help you get started? Do you need a work-table or something?"

Hmm. "That might be useful. Something to put my tools on." I hadn't really given it much thought, but the ground is a perfectly good surface and would have been fine.

Micah turns and walks off, and I lay my suitcase down and open it. My tools are neatly packed inside, exactly the way they were when I zipped the case closed earlier, and I leave them there and step closer to the wall, trying to assess what I'll need first.

My headlamp.

I go back to the suitcase and find the container I put it in to prevent any damage in transit. I used to use a desk lamp, but I have a habit of leaning in close to whatever I'm working on and blocking the light. A headlamp ended up being a more sensible solution, because leaning closer just means more light.

I slip the band onto my head, adjust it until it's comfortable, and turn it on. Then I return to the wall.

Much better.

Dragon magic is seriously badass, if this is all the rust that's managed to develop after thousands of years. I can't wait to meet the dragon that's coming to help with whatever we find.

I'm still studying the elements closest to me, trying to see if there are signs that show which components will fit to each one, when a hand lands on my shoulder. I screech, spin around with my hands coming up to defend me, and promptly trip over the damn boots.

Luckily, Micah catches me before I collide with the wall. Some of those protruding metal bits could cause serious damage. "Easy," he says. "Be careful until we can get you some shoes that fit."

I don't bother to point out that it's not going to make much difference. If he hasn't learned that already, it'll be a nice surprise for him.

Instead, I lean against his chest, inhaling the scent of him, and say, "Didn't anyone ever teach you not to sneak up on people like a creepy serial killer?"

"I called your name five times," he informs me. For the barest second, he rests his cheek against the top of my head. "Come and tell me if you want your tools arranged in any specific way."

I lift my head and look past him. He's set up a trestle table beside my suitcase. There's a folding chair next to it, with his tablet on the seat.

"Where did they come from?" I take a cautious step, maintain my balance, and follow it up with a few more.

"Zac made a list of shit that might be needed and made us bring it all up here the other day. Most of it's over there." He waves to the area behind the lights. They're pointed at the wall, so it's kind of shadowy back there. "If there's anything you need, let me know. It might already be here."

"That's smart." And organized in a way I'll never manage. I might make the list, but then I'd probably lose it.

We spend a couple minutes laying my tools out in the order I think I'll need them. They'll all be jumbled together within a day or so, but at least I'm starting with good intentions. Then I clomp over to the crates. There are symbols on the lids, but they mean nothing to me. "Which is the first one?" It's not going to help if I start at the wrong end.

"Here." Micah, who was hovering behind me with every step like some kind of nervous chaperone, guides me along the rows. "We laid them out in the order they were stacked. This was the top row. The elf who translated the symbols said this one"—he lays a hand on one—"is first. That's second," he adds, pointing.

I nod. "Okay. Not to be a ballbreaker, but I want to look in every crate before I get started. And can we number them in a language I recognize? Like with a Post-it or something? I don't want to risk that I'll get them mixed up later."

"Of course," he says confidently, prying the lid off the first crate. "Start here while I get a pen."

I'm already leaning over the crate as he walks away, shining my headlamp onto the components inside. There are five different ones, and I pick up one, holding it close to my face to examine it.

"Huh."

"What?" Micah asks, and I jump.

"What did I *just* tell you about doing that?"

"Sorry. What were you huh-ing about?"

I tip my head back to look him in the eye. "Is that even a word?"

He reaches out and turns off my headlamp, which was shining directly into his eyes. Oops. "Is what even a word?"

"Huh-ing."

"I have no idea what you just said."

"No, it was you who said it." Wasn't it? I'm pretty sure. I'd remember if I made up a word.

Maybe.

"Let's start again," he suggests, and he doesn't sound impatient like most people who say that to me do. Instead, there's a tiny—so tiny I might need to turn my headlamp back on to confirm it—smile on his lips. It's so weird, but I get this feeling he actually likes me.

I mean, after last night, I know he *likes* me. Sex is a talent and a vocation I was born with, and I know when a man's having an excellent time. But that doesn't mean they necessarily like *me*, the person, once the fun times are done. I know my shortcomings. I'm scattered, hyperfocused on puzzles to the detriment of other stuff, and I'm so clumsy, people have joked that I should be wrapped in bubble wrap.

But aside from right after we met, Micah hasn't seemed bothered by any of that. And when he looks at me, it seems like he's glad I'm here. Not me the puzzle expert—just me. Cam.

I gaze up at him and wonder if I'm reading too much into

this. Maybe he's just a super patient person and I haven't had enough time to annoy him yet. That's cool. I'll be here for a couple of months. That's plenty of time to wear on his every nerve.

"What were you thinking when I interrupted you?" he asks.

I blink a few times. "I don't remember." Dammit. What if it was important?

Micah's not fazed, though. He takes my hand and lifts it. I'm still holding one of the components from inside the crate. "You were looking at this, and something made you go huh."

Oh! "Yeah, that's right! Thanks, Micah. You're the best." I turn toward the crate to grab another component, but he gently turns me back to face him.

"So what was it?"

For a second, I wonder what he's talking about, then I realize I never told him what I'd been thinking. Doh! "This component—I can't be completely sure just yet, but I think it has two points at which it could connect to something else."

He frowns, but I'm not scared. Micah wouldn't hurt me. It's not his fault his face is like that. "What does that mean?"

I shrug. "Don't know for sure. It could just be that the designer wanted to make it a little more fun to fit the components. Like, does this end go in, or this one? Add another lot of possibilities for each step."

He eyes me doubtingly. "Or?"

I grin, because this is the exciting part. "Or, it could mean that the components need to fit together too. Another layer of puzzle."

"So one end of the component would fit into an element on the wall, but the other end would need to fit together with one of the components beside it?" He sounds aghast and grudgingly admiring. I wouldn't have thought those were two emotions that could go together, but he pulls it off.

"Yep! Or..." I turn my head and look over the rows of crates thoughtfully. "Did you count how many components are in these?"

"No. We thought it was best not to mess around and risk mixing things up or losing them."

I nod slowly. "I don't think it's worth counting them now. I'd need to count the elements on the wall too, and if everything's in the order that I'll need to use it, like we think, then it's not really going to make a difference anyway."

He frowns again, turning to look first at the wall, then at the crates. "You think there are too many components," he says finally.

"Not too many," I correct. "There are the perfect number for what's needed."

"But you're not sure if what's needed is a single layer of components connected to the elements or a double layer?"

He's so clever. I like a man who can understand what I'm thinking without me having to spell it out.

"The best way to find out is to start solving the puzzle. But I do still want to check in all the crates first." I lean into the first one and grab one each of the other components. Once I'm into the rhythm of the puzzle, I'll bring bunches of them over to my workspace, but until I find the starting point, I won't need more than this. Slipping them all into my pockets—which weighs my pants down a lot—I say, "Let's put the lid back on. I'm not sure if that affects the preservation spell, and I don't want to mess with it."

Micah shrugs. "Whatever you want." He lifts the lid on without needing my help (what does an architect need with those muscles, anyway?) and then tapes an index card to it and writes 1.

I nod approvingly and move toward the next crate, but he grabs my arm. "That's not the second one."

I look at it, then up at him. "It's not?"

He shakes his head.

"Are you sure?"

"Positive."

"Which one is?"

He points. I glance at the alleged second crate, then around at all the others. Dammit. If crate one is at the top left corner of a grid, it does make sense for that to be the second one. Somehow I got turned around.

"Good job." I pat him on the chest and step over to the second crate.

"Did you just pat me like a dog?"

I can't tell if he's amused or offended. "Not like a dog. Like a... clever demon."

He mutters something I don't quite hear, then pries the lid off the second crate for me. I sneak a peek at his face, trying to see if he's mad. He gazes steadily back at me.

"If you need to do some work, I'll be fine here," I venture, but he shakes his head.

"I cleared today to be at your service."

Ohhhhhh, baby. Those are words I love to hear.

# CHAPTER TWELVE

## Micah

We're barely back in the teleport room in Cam's house when his phone goes nuts. The chimes are practically falling over each other, and they go on for a good twenty seconds. I raise a brow at him. "Someone misses you."

He frowns as he hauls his phone out of his pocket. "I've got no idea who." He glances at the screen and rolls his eyes. "Oh, for fuck's sake."

"Problem?" He seems more exasperated than concerned, so I'm not worried. I take a step toward the door.

"Nah, just this asshat who won't get a life and leave me alone."

Midstep, I freeze. "What?"

Cam breezes past me. "Do we have time for a shower before we go to dinner? I'm glad you and Garrett made me borrow this coat. The cave didn't seem that cold, but after a few hours, it seeps into your bones, doesn't it?"

I reach out and snag the back of said coat before he can get too far away from me. "Come back here."

"What?" He looks over his shoulder, face a study of confused innocence.

"There's someone blowing up your phone who won't leave you alone?"

He blows a raspberry. "Him? He's a pest."

I let go of the jacket and take his shoulders in my hands, turning him to face me. He blinks up at me from under his mop of curls. "What kind of pest? Ex-boyfriend?"

"No, nothing like that. I guess you could call him a disgruntled client? He ordered something a few years back, but then tried to weasel out of paying. Since then, he's been a low-key annoyance."

Something about the whole situation seems off to me, but Cam's not worried, so I tell myself to let it go. Acting all overbearing isn't going to convince him to sleep with me again, and that's a lot higher on my priority list than some random former client of his. "You should block his number," I suggest, letting go of him. He immediately turns for the door.

"I tried that. He just texts from another phone. I— Yaaahhh!"

I lunge forward, but he's too far into the hall for me to catch him this time. Fortunately, he stumbles shoulder-first into the wall and manages to avoid hitting his head.

"Are you okay?" I gather him in my arms and tilt his chin upward. "You didn't hit your head, did you?" It doesn't hurt to double-check. His eyes are focused and clear, but signs of concussion don't always show up immediately.

"Just my shoulder. And it's fine." His voice is a little breathy as he gazes at me.

"Are you sure? Rotate your arm."

He makes a sound that shoots straight to my dick. "Are we going to play doctor? I can be a good patient, Doctor."

I'm literally speechless... and way more turned on than I expected to be. "Uhhh..."

He bats his eyelashes and strips off his coat and sweater

right there in the hallway. "Maybe you could kiss it better for me?"

My gaze drops to his torso. The pale skin gleams in the low lighting, goose bumps rising as the air hits it after being wrapped up warm. Old bruises splotch his arms, and there's one on his hip, rising from the waistband of his pants. It looks new. "When did this happen?" I ask, tracing it lightly with a single finger. He shivers.

"I walked into a crate."

I frown. Clearly I'm going to need to keep a better eye on him. Crouching, I lay my lips against it in a barely there kiss, then raise my eyes to his. "Better?"

He swallows hard. "A little."

"Hmm." I stand, then lean down and whisper my lips along his shoulder. It's red where he hit the wall, but not bruised yet. "What about this? Does it help at all?"

"S-sure. But I think the treatment might need to be repeated. A few times."

I smile against his skin and skim down his arm to the next bruise. This one, I lick.

His whole body shudders. I don't know if it's because his arm is an erogenous zone or if it's something else, but this is really working for him.

Good.

Straightening, I back him into the wall and take his lips in a deep, hungry kiss. He tastes like the candy he's been sucking on all day, and the scent of machine oil and soap rises around me, sexier than any designer cologne could hope to be. He kisses me back eagerly, hitching one leg over my hip and hoisting himself higher against my body. I grab his round ass in my hands and let him grind all over me. Our clothes are a curse between us, and in just one second, I'm going to break this kiss to get them off.

In a few seconds...

Just a few—

He pulls away, and I'm chasing him with my mouth before I realize he's speaking.

"... get that? This is the third time it's rung."

The real world crashes back in, and I hear my phone ringing. If it's Zac, I swear I'm going to tell Grandmother that he's lonely and wants help meeting people.

The ringing stops, and I lean in toward Cam. "I guess it's not important," I murmur, only to be cockblocked when it starts again. "Fuck!"

He laughs. "Come on, put me down. I'm getting hungry anyway. Answer it, and then we'll go to dinner."

How can he think of food at a time like this? I'm hungry too, but not for whatever Garrett's cooking.

My disgruntlement must be obvious, because he leans forward and plants a kiss on my mouth. "Don't frown at me. I know you're only grumpy on the outside. Put me down, and I promise we can have shower sex later." He pauses. "I'm *gifted* with body wash."

I don't doubt that at all.

Regretfully, I put him back on his feet, wait a second to make sure he's steady, and then pull out my phone. It's ringing *again*. "What?" I snarl.

"Don't what me," Asher growls. "Garrett cooked, and you're a rude asshole. Get over here and show my husband proper appreciation for his hard work."

I roll my eyes. Garrett's great, but the way Asher worships him, you'd think small forest animals came to do his chores. "We got held up, but we're on our way." I glance at Cam, who's putting his sweater on inside out. "Five minutes."

Asher's talking when I hang up on him. I do it deliberately, of course. He thinks that because he's the oldest of our little group of cousins, that gives him authority over the rest of us. I like to keep him humble.

"Not like that," I warn Cam, stopping him before he can pull the sweater over his head. I free his arms from it and turn it the right way out. "Okay, now try."

He sighs in exasperation and consternation. "Not again. That happens to me way too often."

I can't help smiling. He stops with one arm in the sweater and smiles back. "You're so understated," he says randomly.

"I am?" I don't even know what that means.

He nods. "Yeah. Most of the time I don't know what you're thinking or feeling because your face is like..." He makes a stone face. "But then sometimes I see you smile, and it's nice."

Oh, I get it. "We demons have more subtle facial expressions than other species," I explain. "Teleporting takes a lot of energy, so we have denser muscle mass, and it doesn't react the same way yours does."

His jaw drops, sweater forgotten. "I had no idea! I've been around demons before—I mean, not much, but still—and I just never knew."

"When we're around other species, we try to exaggerate things like smiles and frowns so you can see them better. I guess I'm out of the habit, living here with only demons. I'll try harder."

"No." He puts his free hand on my chest. "You don't have to. I like it this way—it feels like I've won something when I make you smile big enough for me to notice."

Warmth spreads from his hand through my torso, and I find myself grinning.

"See! Like that. I did that. Besides, you shouldn't have to change to make me more comfortable. I'll learn to spot the subtle expressions." He pauses and tips his head. "Well, I'll try. But I'll probably get distracted and forget or just not notice."

"If it's something you need to know, I'll use words," I tell him dryly. Because even though it's only been a little over twenty-four hours since we met, I'm absolutely sure he'll get distracted and not notice. "Put your sweater on."

He looks down at the forgotten clothing dangling from one arm. "Oh. Good idea."

While he's getting dressed, I think disgusting thoughts in an attempt to chase away the remnants of my boner. My cousins will never let me hear the end of it if I held up dinner because I was horny. They probably suspect, but I'm not going to confirm it for them.

Two minutes later, we're sitting down to dinner while Cam apologizes earnestly to Garrett for the delay. "I had some bruises Micah needed to check."

Garrett frowns a little. "Are you okay? There isn't a doctor or sorcerer healer in town, but Micah can take you to Zurich."

Zac coughs, and Asher outright smirks. Assholes.

"I'm fine. They weren't that bad," Cam assures him. "This smells great!"

It really does. Lasagna is a definite crowd pleaser around here. We dig in, and I hadn't realized how hungry—for food —I was until the first bite hits my stomach. Silence reigns while we take the edge off.

"So," Zac says when I fork up the last mouthful and look around for seconds. "Grandmother called me this afternoon."

Asher and I pause. "She called me too," he says slowly, putting his fork down. "Did she ask you a bunch of questions?"

Zac nods.

"She didn't call me, but I saw her this morning. What was

her mood like for you?" I ask. She seemed to be in a better frame of mind by the end of the meeting, but still not what I would have considered optimal. Sometimes it's important to remind ourselves that she really does love us a lot.

"She was cheerful," Zac replies immediately, and Asher agrees. Garrett freezes midway in serving Asher another piece of lasagna.

"Cheerful?" he repeats. "Are you sure?"

"It's pretty hard to mistake it when Grandmother is cheerful," Asher tells him dryly. "It doesn't happen all that often."

"Except around the kids," Zac adds. "She's usually cheerful with them."

That's true. She likes little kids. Which reminds me, I need to visit my brother. I promised to introduce him to Cam.

"But she was in a lousy mood this morning," Garrett protests, dumping lasagna on Asher's plate with no finesse. "Definitely did *not* roll out the welcome mat for Cam. What could have happened to change that?"

"I liked her," Cam says, holding out his plate for more. "And she did welcome me. She invited me for dinner on Sunday." He looks around the table with a frown. "I don't have to go if it will be weird, though."

"I already told you it won't," I remind him. "She invited you, so unless you don't want to come, you're coming."

"She invited you for family dinner?" Zac lets out a low whistle. "She must have liked you. That also explains why she was asking so many questions about you and if I thought you were nice."

"Did she?" Cam grins. "She does like me! Maybe I should bring her a present on Sunday. Does she like puzzles?"

There's a very good chance that she'd throw a metal

puzzle through a window if she couldn't work out how to solve it, but that's not what he's asking. "She does."

"Great! What did you tell her, Zac? Did you say I was nice?"

Zac smiles indulgently at him. "I told her you're adorable."

# CHAPTER THIRTEEN

## Cam

It's so nice to wake up in a warm bed with my very own personal demon heater snuggled against me. Micah has his arm wrapped around me and my body tucked into his, as though he's protecting me from the... cold? Blanket? Who knows. But it's nice. I haven't had this—someone to snuggle and wake up with—for a long time. Most people get bored when I start talking about work and only stick around for the actual fucking. Others stick around for a while but then get frustrated when they realize how much of my attention goes to puzzles and how little I want to go to parties. Unless they're trivia parties. I've been to a few of those, and they're so much fun, even if I don't know the answers.

I wonder if the pub Micah mentioned, here in the village, does trivia parties.

Micah stirs behind me, nuzzling the back of my neck. "Good morning," he rumbles. "What are you thinking about so loudly?"

"Was I talking?" How embarrassing. "Good morning. I hope I didn't wake you."

He gently bites my ear, and I shiver. "Not talking, but you weren't relaxed anymore."

And he noticed that in his sleep? Is that a demon superpower, or just a Micah thing? "I was wondering if the pub does trivia parties."

"The pub here in the village? Sure. The second Friday of the month. Did you want to go? You should still be here then. We can make up a team—you, me, my cousins, and Garrett."

How exciting! I sit up, and only when the covers fall to my waist do I realize how fucking cold it is. Yelping, I dive for the warmth of the blankets, accidentally elbowing Micah in the ribs as I do.

"Oof!" Even as he presses a hand to his side, he gathers me close with his other arm. "What's wrong?"

I burrow against his chest, yanking the covers up to my chin. "It's freezing!"

His laugh vibrates through me. "The heat is programmed to turn down at night, but it's definitely not freezing. Trust me. The heating system never lets the house get below fifty-five."

"Fifty-five? That's freezing. Okay, well maybe not *technically*," I concede. "But it's colder than my naked body wants to be." I make my eyes as big and pleading as I can. "Turn up the thermostat for me? Please?"

He laughs again, and I wallow in the sound. I made this clever, handsome man laugh like that, all warm and indulgent. If I'd known that working away from home came with benefits like this, I'd have done it sooner.

"What time is it?" he asks. "The thermostat is programmed to warm the house up from six on weekdays and seven on weekends. It should kick in soon."

I wriggle around in his arms until my back is to him, then reach out and snag my phone from the nightstand. "It's six fifty,"

I announce. "I guess we'll just have to stay in bed until the house warms up. Oh no. Poor me. Snuggled in bed with a sexy demon on a Saturday morning. How will I survive?" I push my ass back into his groin. His morning wood is nice and hard, and a certain muscle clenches just at the memory of how it felt inside me.

"We could play games on our phones," he suggests, his hand sliding down my belly to firmly grasp my cock.

"Games sound like fun," I agree, a little breathlessly, "but I read this article that says using technology in bed is bad for you." Or something. I'm sure an article like that exists.

"I think we have an old edition of Monopoly somewhere," he teases.

"I've already passed Go and need to move on to one of the overpriced hotels."

His chuckle is a breath against my neck. "I guess the only other thing to do is talk quietly. Or maybe take a nap."

"Mi-cah..." I whine, and he finally relents.

"Pass me the lube."

⟡

Bundled up warmly in the clothes Micah helped me get—including the cute scarf he ordered without me knowing, in a really cool random geometric pattern that's almost like a puzzle—I wander along the main street of Hortplatz. The wind is barely there today, nothing like the other night, and even though it's still cold and cloudy, there are plenty of people around.

"It didn't use to be so busy on the streets," Micah says when he sees me looking around. "Mostly because they were covered in snow. This is all Garrett's doing—now that we're trying to make the village attractive to other species, we need them to be able to walk around."

I try to make sense of that. "You mean there was nowhere for people to walk?"

He shakes his head. "What did we need that for? If there's snow in the way, we'd just teleport to wherever we were going. But this is nice—stretching our legs, getting fresh air. And Zoe's snow village is amazing."

"Snow village?" If that's what it sounds like, I want to see it.

"I'll show you later. We'll loop around that way. Now, this is the grocery store. I know you don't cook, but—"

"The place of snacks," I interrupt. "Do they have ready meals too?"

"Only the frozen kind. But don't worry about that—we'll keep you fed." His smile is a subtle little one. He's been cooking for me or taking me to his house to eat all week, and it seems that he likes that.

We go into the grocery store. It's not that different to home, except for the brands and some of the types of food. Like, there aren't any PopTarts, but I'm not mad about the kajillion different cheeses they stock. Cheese makes everything better.

"Micah," a voice calls while I'm inspecting a piece of cheese labeled Sbrinz, which Micah assures me I'd like. I mean, duh.

We turn toward the newcomer, an older-middle-aged demon wearing a shirt with the store's logo on it and a big smile. "Is this the puzzle expert? Welcome! I'm Griff. If there's anything you need that's not in stock, just let me know. Our special order process is much faster than what you're used to." He winks, which is... weird. But I just smile and nod enthusiastically. Maybe he means it's a lot faster for demons to teleport somewhere and pick up a special order than it is for other species.

"That's so kind. Thank you! But you have a great range

here, and I'm sure I won't need anything else. I love how much cheese there is."

His face lights up like I've just told him he won the lottery. "Yes, we have lots of cheese! Most of what we stock is locally made, except the ones like Stilton that need to be imported."

"Micah's showing me around the village right now, but I'll be back later for cheese and other snacks," I promise. "Do you have chocolate milk?"

Griff seems a little surprised but nods. "Of course. But... the cheese and chocolate milk together... you might get a stomachache?"

What an excellent point.

"Don't worry, Griff," Micah assures him. "He'll have them separately."

That seems to relieve Griff. "I'll set up an account for you," he tells me. "When you're ready, just tell the cashier to put it on your account." He pats my shoulder and walks away before I can ask if he needs my credit card or anything.

"That's very trusting of him," I say quietly to Micah as we leave.

He shrugs. "It's not like you can leave town in the dead of night. Besides, he knows that if you tried to skip out without paying, I'd cover it. Or Grandmother would."

I frown. That's not right. "You're not responsible for my debts. I can pay my own way."

Micah smiles at me and hooks his arm through mine. "Great. Pay for your groceries before you leave town, and there won't be a problem."

That sounds logical and reasonable, but I still don't like that the town apparently considers Micah my guarantor. I've been supporting myself for over a hundred years, and from what I've heard, the village council already expects his time for free. It's not right that they should expect his money too.

I'm still stewing over that when Micah leads me into the pub. It's charming—all exposed beams and warm brass fixtures. One wall is all glass doors leading out onto a terrace, though they're closed today against the cold. A giant fireplace dominates the back wall, and I can feel the warmth of the fire from here.

I turn to Micah. "Can we come back here tonight? For dinner, maybe? They do dinner, right?"

"We do," the man behind the bar calls, even as he pulls beer from a tap for a waiting patron. "Micah, is this the puzzle man?"

Micah introduces me to Arne, the publican, and also to three other people currently at the bar. Arne tells us the special tonight is Älplermagronen and promises to hold a table for us for dinner. I don't know what that is, but from the way Micah smiles, I'll probably like it.

Next we head toward the snow village. (I did walk into a chair in the pub while Micah was saying goodbye, but neither I nor the chair are hurt.)

"Tell me again what this snow village is," I prompt as we stroll.

"Exactly what it sounds like," he replies. "We've told you about Zoe?"

"The sorcerer who moved up here to help clear the snow?" I'm pretty sure that's what they said.

"Yes. We have a snowplow too, but Zoe's expertise is essential. It was her idea to not just dump the snow in huge drifts around the village. Instead, she uses it to make more family-friendly outdoor winter spaces. Like there." He points to a park. There are some trees, but most of the space is taken up by a pond.

"The skating pond?" There are plenty of people zipping over the ice like it's normal to strap knives to your feet and then balance on them. Not that I've ever achieved that level of balance.

"That's not a pond. It's firmly compacted snow, plus a little water, plus Zoe's sorcery skill. That turned it into a thick sheet of ice safe for skating on."

My mouth forms an O. "Impressive. Is she looking for a bestie who thinks ice puzzles would be the coolest thing ever?"

He tugs me along. "Wait until you see the snow village."

We reach the edge of the village, where the road kind of peters out into a path that isn't plowed. Ahead, I can see fir trees, enough of them that I'd refer to that area as "the woods." Micah points. "In summer, you can follow that path up above the tree line. The cave is up there."

"My cave?" I squint in that direction. I can't even see above the tree line—the clouds are too low. I know there's a peak over there, because I've seen it before, but not today.

"Yours?" He leans down to kiss my cheek. "Don't let Grandmother hear you say that."

Before I can argue that it really *is* my cave—for a little while, at least—we round a corner, and I gasp.

Because dead ahead is the cutest damn snow village I've ever seen in my life.

The buildings are all kid-sized, and I'm guessing only one room inside, but the detail is amazing. There are roads, lampposts, mailboxes, and houses, with windowsills and imitation-slate-tiled roofs. Small snow people are even loitering on street corners, and one is leaning out an upstairs window. Village kids are running around the whole area, going in and out of buildings and pretending to play shopkeeper and a dozen other things.

"Pretty special, yes?" Micah asks. I can feel his gaze on me, but I can't look away from the snow village. Everywhere my eyes land, there's something new to see.

"Zoe's a genius."

"Did I hear my name?"

I turn—reluctantly—to see a tall blonde woman walking toward us. She's dressed for the weather but somehow looks like she should be on a catwalk. And even with the muffler wrapped around her neck and covering her lower face, I can tell she's smiling.

Sticking out my hand, I say, "I'm Cam, and if you're Zoe, you're *amazing*."

She shakes my hand. "I *am* Zoe. And if you're the guy who's going to solve the puzzle in the cave and jump-start the tourism industry here so I can do this"—she sweeps her arm toward the snow village—"every year, then I think you're amazing too."

I look back at the mock village. The joy on the kids' faces as they play. The smiles of their parents as they stand nearby, sipping from thermoses and takeout cups and chatting sociably. This is definitely something that should happen every year.

"They can just call us the amazing twins, then."

# CHAPTER FOURTEEN

## Cam



"Tell me again who's going to be there?" I demand, stepping away from the hand Micah was about to put on my arm. He sighs. This is the third time I've delayed us from teleporting to his grandmother's house. It's not that I'm nervous, but more that I'm... concerned. Sure, Damaris seemed cranky and kinda hardcore in the meeting the other day, but she was also fair. I can handle that. But then her grandsons and Garrett got all freaked out about her, and now I'm concerned.

A smart man knows when to be concerned.

Micah gives me that look, the one that says he knows what I'm doing but thinks I'm adorable anyway. I've quickly come to like that a lot. Most people give me the "how can you get on my nerves this much" look instead.

"You and me," he says, not for the first time, "Asher, Garrett, and Zac. My grandmother. My parents and brother, Asher's parents and sister, and Zac's mother."

I nod as though it's the first time I've heard it. "And you're sure the kids like puzzles?"

"They do. If you show them how they work, they'll adore you," he promises patiently.

"And your grandmother—"

"My grandmother is very appreciative of anything crafted by hand. If she knows you made the puzzle, she'll be extremely grateful."

I guess I don't have any more reasons to delay. Oh, wait. "You're sure what I'm wearing is okay?"

He smiles. It's a tiny one, but I'm getting better at spotting them. "It's time to go, Cam." He puts an arm firmly around my shoulders and teleports us out of there.

The room we arrive in is the same as every other teleport room I've seen so far: bare except for a poster on the wall. This one at least is painted a nice teal color, with white trim. If Damaris went to the trouble of choosing a pretty paint color for a room nobody spends time in, she can't be that bad.

Micah opens the door and calls, "Anybody home?" The resulting cries of excitement and running feet make me curious, and I follow him into the hall.

Two kids come racing toward us. The girl, who looks a little older, skids to a stop, but the boy barrels into Micah's legs. "Hi! You said you were going to bring the puzzle man to visit me!"

Aww. That's so cute.

Micah bends down and lifts the kid into his big, strong arms. I wonder if it would be inappropriate for me to fan myself. "I did. Here he is. This is Cam. Cam, meet Chloe and Isaac."

Both kids look at me. The little boy gets suddenly shy and buries his face in his brother's shoulder. "Hi." I give an awkward little wave. "I brought you something."

When in doubt, bribe.

Isaac's little head comes up immediately. "A present?" He wriggles to be put down. Micah obliges with a snort.

"I thought you might like some puzzles. I made them just for you." I reach into my coat and pull out the two simpler puzzles I made. I don't do a lot of kid stuff anymore, since most parents aren't willing to pay custom rates for them, but I always enjoy them when I do. It's almost more difficult to come up with something that's creative and going to challenge them without being too hard. Handing them the plain cotton pouches, I say, "I can show you how they work, but if you want to try by yourself first, that would be fun."

"Thank you," Chloe says by rote. She opens the pouch, and her mouth forms an O. "It looks like a robot," she breathes.

"Yep. And when it's all solved, it will look like a smiley face."

Isaac's eyes get all big, and he opens his pouch. The two puzzles are the same, since I didn't want to risk any arguments over them. I might not spend much time with kids anymore, but I remember what it can be like. "Mine's a robot too," he says, then looks up at me with a grin. He must be thrilled, because I can see it clearly, not tiny at all. "Thank you!" He throws his arms around my legs for a quick hug, then races back down the hall, yelling, "Look what the puzzle man brought me!" Chloe chases after him.

I meet Micah's gaze. "I'm going to be 'the puzzle man' forever, aren't I?"

He cocks a brow. "We both know you love that idea."

The grin that takes over my face is totally involuntary. "Yeah."

A figure appears at the end of the hallway: tall, masculine, looks a lot like Micah. "Are you planning to join us, son?"

Is this Micah's dad? At least Micah knows what he'll look like in the future: good.

"We're coming," Micah says, giving me a little nudge to start me moving. I've noticed he does that—makes me go first so he can keep an eye on me and catch me if I lose my balance. A few times yesterday, while he was showing me around town, he redirected me before I could bump into something. It's nice having someone watch out for me, and it makes me feel special that he's choosing to do it. I gave him an extra-good blowjob last night to show my gratitude.

I get to where the older demon is standing and stop. His face is that typical demon mask, but he has kind eyes. Or maybe I'm just projecting because his eyes are like Micah's. Micah's are like his? Whatever.

I hold out a hand. "Hi. I'm Cam Torrence. Thanks for your son."

He blinks twice and looks over my shoulder at Micah. "You're welcome?"

"He's been a huge help," I continue blithely. "But he's also just a really nice guy. He looks after me, you know? Even stuff he doesn't have to do."

Micah's dad smiles, and it's not a subtle demon one. It's wide and warm, and the look he gives Micah this time is affectionate. "He's a good boy. I've always been proud of him. I'm Hal Bailey, by the way."

"It's nice to meet you. I gave Isaac a puzzle—I hope that's okay. Micah said it was." Too bad if I've just thrown him under a bus.

"Micah was right. Although, it's not going to save you from the millions of questions Isaac has. He's been excited to meet you ever since he heard you were coming."

Someone calls his name from the room behind him, and he turns his head, then looks back at me with a smile— smaller, this time. If I wasn't looking for it, I wouldn't have seen it. "Come on. Mother's getting impatient."

We enter a huge living room. The entire back wall is glass, with the most stupendous view of the mountains, and I stagger to a stop so I can gape at them for a moment.

"Special, isn't it?" Micah murmurs, stopping beside me. "See that peak there, the closest one?"

"The one that looks like it's looming over us?"

"That's the one. The cave's up there, just above the tree line."

Wow. Suddenly I'm glad I don't need to walk there and back every day. I drag my eyes away from the peaks, and they land on Damaris. She's watching me, her face demon-blank. I can't read anything in her eyes either.

Gathering all my courage, I cross the room toward her. For once, Micah doesn't follow, and I really wish he had. After he and his cousins—who are also here—spent all that time making me second-guess my impression of their grandmother, the least he can do is support me while I talk to her.

I come to a stop a few steps away from her and muster a smile. "Thank you for inviting me today. Your home is lovely." Not that I've seen much of it. But these windows are stupendous. "I really like the color you painted the teleport room."

The lines around her eyes soften a little. She doesn't do anything as obvious as smile, but she does seem pleased by the compliment. "Just because we don't spend a lot of time in there doesn't mean it can't be attractive," she says, and I nod.

"Definitely. I hope you don't mind, but I brought this for you." I offer her the cotton pouch with a puzzle in it. "Just a small token of my work."

"How kind of you." She takes it and opens the pouch. The puzzle is pretty stock-standard, good for a beginner but not so easy that it's boring. "This will keep me busy, I'm sure."

She's not offended—not that I thought she would be. I mean, who doesn't appreciate a present?—and that's good enough for me.

"Come and meet the family," she says, turning me toward them. "I believe you already know my grandsons? And Garrett, of course."

"They've been very welcoming, and have generously fed

me," I assure her. The satisfied vibe I get in return is... weird. She's glad her family is feeding me?

Not that I think she wants me to starve, but it's not usually something you take pleasure from... right?

I'm so busy thinking about it that I trip and stumble into poor Zac. He catches me and helps me get my balance back.

"I'm so sorry." My face gets hot. Micah's cousins have seen me be my usual clumsy self, but I've never nearly knocked one of them over. Plus, this isn't an ideal introduction to the rest of the family.

"Don't worry about it," Zac assures me with a friendly pat on the arm. "There are worse things than having a man practically fall at my feet."

I laugh along with them all, relieved I haven't made too big an idiot of myself. Garrett sidles up beside me.

"I saw you talking to Micah's dad before, but come and meet his mom and Asher's parents," he suggests, looping an arm through one of mine.

"Oh—no, Garrett, I need to speak with you," Damaris says, so quickly she almost stumbles over the words. "Zac will introduce Cam to everyone."

"I can introduce myse—" I begin, but she interrupts me.

"Micah will get you a drink. We'll be having dinner soon, so just chat and enjoy. Zac will take care of you. Come, Garrett." She turns away, clearly expecting her instructions to be followed, and Garrett bugs out his eyes at me before following. I feel like maybe he's trying to convey some kind of message, but I've never been good at understanding signals like that. It's hard enough to concentrate on what people are actually saying, much less try to read their minds.

"Come and meet everyone," Zac says cheerfully. "I promise they only bite on Tuesdays."

"Not Mondays?" I joke halfheartedly. "I'm sorry you got stuck with me." And I really wish he was Micah. I like Zac, but he's not Micah. Meeting strange people in a new place is something I really want Micah with me for.

"No, we're good. I like your company. Say hi to my mom, Dalia. Mom, this is Cam Torrence, who's going to solve the puzzle door and help us lure the community to this town."

The genes in this family run strong. Zac's mom looks like Damaris would have a few hundred years ago, but less... forbidding. Not that she's soft and cuddly, but where I can believe Damaris might put a hit out on someone, Dalia would likely just key their car.

I hope.

"Hello, Cam." She holds out her hand to me. "It's great to meet you. We're all very excited about the cave."

Okay. This, I can talk about. "Not as much as me, probably. This is like all my dreams come true."

She looks at me, her son, and then over our shoulders. I turn and catch a glimpse of Damaris watching us. "Not all your dreams, I hope."

## CHAPTER FIFTEEN

### Micah

Something weird is going on, and I'm not completely sure what it is. It has to do with Cam, though, and that's getting my protective instincts all riled up.

Not that I think anyone here would hurt him—all signs point in the opposite direction. Grandmother's being *too* welcoming, if that's possible.

I give my head a tiny shake. Too welcoming? That's ridiculous. I'm overthinking this. Cam's got me tied up in so many knots, I'm not seeing things clearly.

Except, Garrett keeps giving me these meaningful looks I don't know how to interpret. He and Asher were whispering together earlier, and Asher's been acting strange ever since. First he stared at everyone like he was trying to see what they were thinking, and now he's muttering to himself and looking only at his plate.

"Have you spent much time in the Alps, Cam?" Grandmother asks. It must be the thirtieth question she's directed at him since we sat down, and once again he lowers his fork to reply. At this rate, he'll never get to finish his dinner. I wish I was sitting next to him so I could nudge him to be less polite and keep eating, but one of the weird things was Grandmother instructing us all on where to sit. She's never done that before, but nobody was going to argue with her, so I'm across the table from Cam. Zac's sitting beside him, and I wonder if I can text him to make Cam eat more.

"No, none. This is my first time here. Your view is incredible."

Aunt Dalia clucks her tongue. It's a sound I can't remember her ever making before, and Zac shoots her a strange look. I'm not the only one who's noticed people being weird. "That's a travesty," she declares. "So many people come all the way to Europe and never leave the cities."

"Oh, I've never been to Europe before either," Cam says casually, picking up his fork again. "I'm kind of a homebody."

"You've never been to Europe at all?" Dad asks. "But you're not that young." The community of species has a higher rate of international travel than humans do. Partly because we live so much longer, but also because we tend to be less inclined to the kind of nationalism that leads to people proclaiming their home country "the best" and refusing to consider that other places have something to offer. Demons, of course, travel the most, but even those species that have to rely on mundane transportation like to get out and see new places.

"I'm a hundred and nineteen," Cam volunteers. "So yeah, not that young. I planned to travel, but when it came to actually doing it, there was always something else that got prioritized."

"A puzzle?" I smile a little, inviting him to share the joke, and he laughs.

"A puzzle," he admits. "It was usually a puzzle. Once it was a bunch of them."

"Well," Grandmother interjects, "we're glad a puzzle

brought you here. Perhaps since you've finally made it to Europe, you should do some sightseeing while you're here."

"In winter?" Asher's mom asks doubtfully. "Many of the tourist attractions are closed."

Grandmother and Aunt Dalia glare at her so fiercely, it's a wonder she doesn't turn to ash. But my instincts are screaming at me now—and I'm guessing Zac's too, since he gives me a confused look. I shrug. I have no idea what shenanigans are afoot.

"It's a *wonderful* time to sightsee," Aunt Dalia says through clenched teeth, and Cam scoots his chair back from the table an inch. It's very easy to see Auntie's resemblance to Grandmother at times like these. "There are no lines and no annoying tourists."

Zac shakes his head. "Mom, I don't think—"

"What an excellent idea!" Grandmother almost shouts. "Zac can show you around Europe! Your own *personal* tour guide. He's an expert on the Alps, too, you know."

"I am?" Zac asks, bewildered. "Since when?"

This time, the double-pronged glare is aimed at him. "You know more than anyone else here," his mother points out. "You're the ideal person to escort Cam around the area, show him the sights. Keep him company."

It hits me like a freight train what they're doing, and my mouth drops open.

"Finally!" Garrett shouts, and all eyes turn to him. He flushes red. "Uh... I beg your pardon. I-I... That is... There was food stuck in my teeth, and I was trying to get it out. Finally!"

Awkward silence. He sinks lower in his chair while Asher puts an arm around his shoulders.

"Where do you think you'd like to visit first, Cam?" Grandmother asks, diverting everyone's attention, and Garrett takes advantage of the opportunity to make bug eyes at me. Now I understand what he's been trying to signal—badly—this whole time.

My grandmother and aunt are trying to set Cam up with Zac.

This is a nightmare.

It's no secret to anybody that Grandmother wants us all married and preferably bringing new children into the family as soon as possible. She's determined to see the next generation before she dies, and though it wouldn't surprise anyone if she lived for eternity out of sheer stubbornness, realistically she only has a few hundred years left, max. Given the low fertility rates in the community of species, she's not exaggerating when she says she'll miss out if we don't get a move on.

But the matchmaking has to stop. Last year, she was (thankfully) focused on Asher. It drove him so nuts that he invented a fake boyfriend to distract her with. Okay, maybe I helped a little with that idea. But it definitely wasn't me who decided a marriage of convenience was the best way to get Grandmother off his back—that was all him. Luckily it worked out for the best, and he and Garrett are now sickeningly in love, but it could have gone very wrong. He was willing to take the risk to avoid Grandmother's machinations.

I should have known it was too good to be true when she didn't immediately turn her attention to me. I should have been *prepared* for some kind of fiasco. But no, I was so complacently relieved that she wasn't nagging me like she did Asher, and now *this* has happened. She's trying to set Zac up with my...

My...

Fuck.

I can't very well protest this on the grounds that Cam and I have been no-strings fucking for nearly a week. Definitely not in front of my whole family, including the two kids. So what do I do? Sit here while Grandmother and Aunt Dalia matchmake my... person I'm involved with and my cousin?

Sitting up straighter, I stare fixedly at Zac, willing him to look at me. He and Cam are the only ones who can head this off right now, and I wouldn't want to put Cam in the position of having to say "no" to Grandmother. That's not fair.

Zac, on the other hand, can stand up to her for once. If he'd stop listening attentively to what Cam's saying and *look at me*. Why's he listening so hard anyway? There's not going to be a test. Is he trying to impress Cam with how much attention he's paying to him?

Is killing a cousin truly a crime? Yes, I know, murder is bad. But murdering your cousin who tried to poach your... person you're fucking, that's not as bad as murdering someone who didn't deserve it, right?

I'm still mentally debating that when Zac finally looks at me. He blinks—maybe my face is a little intense right now—and his expression turns questioning. I slide my eyes to Cam, then shake my head.

Zac just looks confused.

So I repeat it.

That doesn't seem to help.

I'm in the middle of the third attempt when Chloe asks, "Micah, are you okay?"

I freeze, then force a smile. "Yes. I'm fine."

She tilts her head. "Are you sure? Why are you making faces?"

"Yeah, Micah? Why are you making faces?" Asher echoes, the asshole. He knows exactly why.

"I'm not making faces," I lie. "I have an itchy nose."

"You can scratch it, you know," Chloe points out.

"Just don't stick your finger up it," Isaac adds. "That's not allowed." He frowns. "But nobody will tell me why. They just say it's not polite."

"It's not polite," I confirm, wishing I was anywhere but here. "I won't stick my finger up my nose."

"Honestly, Micah." Grandmother's scowling at me. "This isn't appropriate dinner table conversation."

There's a story people tell about someone Grandmother used to work with. He annoyed her incessantly, but she tolerated it, until one day, he put his feet on her desk and refused to remove them. He went missing a day later and was never seen again. The story is that Grandmother killed him... though nobody can prove it, of course.

I always thought that was a little farfetched. Kill someone over feet on a desk? Grandmother has a short temper, but she's not a monster. Now, though... now I understand. Now I believe she could have done it. Because her blood runs in my veins, and right at this moment, I would happily kill Zac for being too dense to understand my signals.

And Asher, for making the whole situation so much worse.

"My apologies, Grandmother."

She nods and turns back to Cam. "So it's settled. Zac will personally escort you around Europe on the next few weekends. I think Paris first. He lived there for decades and knows all the best—and most romantic—places."

I can actually see the moment realization hits Zac. His eyes widen, his jaw drops, and he swings his head around to look at me. I make a "see? I was trying to tell you" face.

"Uh, Grandmother, I don't think that will work," he begins, then falters as she and his mother both turn on him.

"Why ever not?" Aunt Dalia asks. "Surely you can spare some time for Cam, who's giving up months of his life to help us."

Zac stutters, utter panic plastered on his face. "I-I just don't think I'm the best choice."

I bite back a groan. They just spent the last ten minutes

talking about why he *would* be the best choice. Some of those reasons were flimsy—very flimsy—but the time to dispute them was then, not now.

"Nonsense." Grandmother's prepared to steamroller us all to get her way if she has to. "You're the perfect choice."

"Maybe Cam doesn't want to spend his weekends racing around Europe," Zac argues desperately. "He'll be working hard all week. Maybe he wants weekends off."

All eyes turn to Cam, and I make a mental note to throttle Zac later for throwing him under a bus like this. Cam, however, seems completely unfazed as he forks up the last mouthful of food on his plate. It's hard to believe this is the same man who was so nervous earlier that he delayed us multiple times.

"Oh, I'd love to see Europe," he declares cheerfully. My gut twists, and despair crosses Zac's face. "But not with Zac."

The whole room freezes. Grandmother draws in a breath, and Aunt Dalia's mouth sets in an offended line.

"Why not Zac?" she demands. "He's handsome, personable, intelligent..."

"He is," Cam agrees. "I like Zac a lot. We're probably going to stay friends after I leave here."

"So why don't you want to see Europe with him?"

"Because I'm sleeping with Micah, and it would be awkward."

That's definitely true. It might even be as awkward as this moment.

The first clue that I might have said the wrong thing comes when Isaac asks, "How come you're sleeping with Micah? Don't you have your own bed? We have a spare room, right, Dad? You could stay with us."

Uh-oh.

Before I can stutter out some excuse, his mother says, "Have you finished your dinner? Why don't you and Chloe go see what's in the cookie jar? Grandmother told me it's been restocked."

Both kids are out of their chairs in seconds, completely distracted from my thoughtless comments. "Excuse us, please," Chloe calls over her shoulder, and then they're gone.

And I'm the center of attention again.

"You're sleeping with Micah?" Damaris asks. Her tone is flat, neutral. She's not happy, but she doesn't sound mad either.

"Um... yeah?" I give him a desperate glance, but his face is unreadable. Or maybe I'm just too off-balance to read it. "Is that not okay?" Crap, I hope I haven't just outed him to his family.

Asher's gay, though—and married to Garrett—and I might have taken forever to realize, but Damaris *was* just trying to set me up with Zac. So if I did out him, I'm a sucky person, but it's not a catastrophe. I hope.

"I wasn't expecting it," she says. "It's not what I'd planned." Her lips purse, and she exchanges a glance with her daughter.

"It would mean starting from scratch for this one," Dalia says, gesturing to Zac. "But we hadn't made any progress for Micah, and this would put us well ahead."

I don't know what to say.

Fortunately, Micah does. "I beg your pardon, Aunt Dalia, but this would be a good time to stop talking."

Someone gasps, and if I wasn't at the center of this whole drama, I'd be looking around for popcorn.

"Micah," Hal warns, but Dalia waves him off.

"I was talking about him as though he wasn't here," she concedes. "I can see why he might not like that."

That's... big of her.

"Can you also see why I—and Zac—might not like that you're apparently trying to plan our lives?"

"Leave me out of this," Zac mumbles beside me, then turns his head and mouths, "I'm so sorry."

I give him a small smile of reassurance. This isn't his fault. And hey, Damaris likes me, after all! Enough that she thinks I'd be a good match for her grandson.

Too bad it wasn't the right grandson. I had to speak up, right? Imagine how weird family gatherings would have been if I stopped fucking Micah and started fucking Zac based on their grandmother's say-so.

Not to mention that I don't want to stop fucking Micah. And as much as I like Zac, the thought of traveling around Europe with him when I could be spending that time with Micah is... meh.

"We just want what's best for you," Damaris is saying. "We want you to be happy."

Micah snorts. "I'm not having this argument with you. I hope this horrifying experience has shown you that you need to back off a bit. You put Cam in a very difficult position."

Damaris's eyes narrow, and for a moment, I fear for Micah's safety. But then she nods. "You're right. Cam, please accept my apologies. We didn't intend to make you uncomfortable."

It's more a demand than a request, but I'm going to take it at face value. As long as I don't have to hook up with Zac, there's no harm done. "That's okay," I assure her. "If I weren't already with Micah, I might even be flattered."

Someone makes a little choking noise, but looking at all the demon-blank faces, I can't tell who. I hope I haven't said the wrong thing again.

Damaris seems fine with it, though, accepting my comment with a nod. "And you being with Micah... what does that entail?"

My whole body erupts into panic. What does she mean? Is she asking for *details* of what Micah and I—

"Grandmother, they've only known each other a week." Surprisingly, it's Asher who comes to my rescue. I assumed he was too busy enjoying the show to want to get involved.

With a flip of one hand, Damaris dismisses that excuse. "A week is plenty of time when you're in love."

Whoa. Whoa, *whoa*, WHOA.

In love?

It's been a week! I love his cock and the way he holds me down in bed, and I love the way he's always looking out for me, but love *him*? It's way too soon to even consider that.

"If Cam and I decide we want to share any information with you, Grandmother, be assured that we will." Micah manages to say that with a straight face, like there's actually a possibility we might discuss our relationship with Damaris. Props to him.

She doesn't seem too pleased. "That puts me in a very awkward position, Micah."

Micah blinks slowly, as though he's trying to process that. "How so?"

"Well, is Cam your boyfriend? A future member of this family? Or just a visitor I barely know? I would be much more formal with a guest than with my future grandson-in-law."

Garrett mouths something, a delighted smile on his face, but I can't make it out. My brain is still stuck on "future grandson-in-law."

It's Zac who answers this time. "You continue to treat him as you have today, only without the invasive interference in his personal life. He's an honored guest in the village and a friend to your grandsons."

Warmth spreads through me. I might have said earlier that I would be friends with Zac after I leave, but it's nice to hear that the sentiment is returned. I've spent a lot of time with Micah's cousins this week, and it's reminded me that I don't actually hate people.

Well, not all people. The right people are fun to hang out with. I'm not easy to be friends with—what with my lack of focus and forgetting things like their existence—but when I do see my friends, I'm always glad to have them.

Damaris mutters something, and based on the way Garrett winces, it's not nice, but she acquiesces. "Very well. We'll speak of something else. Cam, how is progress going in the cave?"

I perk up, relieved we've left talk of my sex life behind and excited that someone's actually asked me about the puzzle. "Excellently. I found the starting point after only one day, which backs up my theory that whoever designed this wanted it to be opened."

Micah laughs—a genuine, out loud laugh.

"What?" I ask. He's been an invaluable help to me in these early days. The first stages of solving a complex puzzle are always harder, as I learn the vagaries and tricks of it.

"Tell them what else you found."

I'm not sure what... oh. "You mean the thing about it being a layered puzzle?"

He taps his nose and smiles at me. It feels like an inside joke for just me and him.

"A layered puzzle?" Asher's dad asks. "What's that?"

"Really exciting!" I hold up my hands to demonstrate. "The wall is the base puzzle, and all the things sticking out of it are elements. Each element needs a specific component in order to unlock and allow me to move on to the next element. We already knew that before I got here. But this week I realized that's not all of it. There's another layer of components that go on top of the first layer!"

The silence that follows is familiar to me. It happens a lot when I start talking about puzzles.

"How would that work, exactly?" Dalia is frowning, but it's not a scary frown. It's thoughtful.

I beam, thrilled about the question. "There are two ways. The most common is for the entire first layer of components to be in place and then the second layer built from there. So with the first layer, I need to work out which component fits where, and then which way the element moves in order to unlock. Or vice versa," I add, because I made the happy discovery this week that the wall puzzle has both options. It really is so much fun. "Then when the second layer goes down, it usually happens the opposite way. The layers almost act as two separate puzzles that just happen to connect."

"And the other way?"

"That's what we've got. It's fully integrated—the element won't unlock until both components are fitted. That means that for each element, the number of possible combinations is more than we thought at first."

Hal smiles at me. "You seem very happy about all this. Isn't it more work for you?"

I shrug. "Kinda, but I love it. I really wish I could have met the designer. They must have been awesome."

"From what I've been told, she died a long time ago," Damaris says gently—well, gently for her. "But if you're right about her wanting it to be solved, the dragons will likely be eager to see it when it's done. Perhaps they will be able to tell you about her."

Dragons. "I get to meet multiple dragons?" I try to sound casual. I'm cool. I'm not fizzing with excitement.

"We had a call from the wing leader's security person on Friday," Damaris informs me. "They've found someone who can come and go through the contents of the cave, once the door is open. They wanted to know if he could come early and see some of the process of the puzzle solving also."

"What?" Micah asks. "Why didn't you tell us?"

Damaris raises a brow. "I believe I just did."

"But it's been two days," Asher adds, then looks at his husband. "Did you know this?" The guilty expression on Garrett's face is answer enough. "Why didn't you say anything?"

"The council asked me not to until they'd made a decision," he protests. "Not my fault."

"Until they'd made a decision?" Zac gapes at Damaris. "You were going to tell the dragons they couldn't come early?"

No way. I feel my eyes getting wide. Why would anyone want to say no to dragons?

"We needed to consider the matter carefully. We know very little about the dragons and what their needs would be. It has already been a steep learning curve—and an expensive one—to have non-demon species in the village. Causing harm or offense to dragons because we weren't able to make them comfortable would be a catastrophe."

It sounds good on the surface, but kind of weak when I actually think about it. Looking around the table, nobody else seems convinced either.

"Well," Asher says, clearly not willing to call her a liar, "have you made a decision?"

"After consultation with Gideon, and Garrett's cousin, yes. A party of dragons will be arriving in a week. They will stay for a few days, and then most will leave and one will remain for the duration of the project."

Excitement thrills through me. "Dragons," I breathe.

Garrett grins at me. "Alistair said they're looking forward to meeting you. Apparently one of them loves mechanical puzzles, and Al gave him one of yours."

I freeze. "What?" A dragon has one of my puzzles and wants to meet me? "How?"

He shrugs. "I don't know the details. Alistair was babbling on like he usually does, and I had other stuff to do, so I didn't ask. But you could call him."

I nod three times fast. I'm definitely going to call him.

Micah meets my gaze, and I smile so wide, my cheeks hurt. "Dragons," I tell him.

"They're going to be so impressed by you," he promises. "Just wait and see."

When he says it, I almost believe it might be true.

# CHAPTER SEVENTEEN

## Micah

I love watching Cam work. He doesn't need my help so much now that he's all set up, so it gives me more time to focus on my own work... and watch him.

Right now, he has this look of utter concentration on his face as he manipulates a component. His hair flops over his forehead, and he swipes it away, leaving a small streak of grease in its place. The wall has been preserved incredibly well, but he discovered within the first few days that there was a definite need for some parts to be oiled. He was a little worried that it might need some kind of specific dragon oil, but I managed to convince him to try the regular kind first, since it's unlikely the dragons brought any special kind of oil with them when they fled their homeworld. Fortunately, the stuff he uses on his other puzzles worked just fine.

The component must click into place, because he steps back and grins. It still makes me nervous when he does that, even though we've been at this for nearly two weeks. Initially, he asked for a ladder so he could reach the higher elements. That lasted exactly four minutes before he hooked one leg over a rung and leaned so far to the side that the ladder toppled. If I didn't have the ability to teleport, he'd have fallen eight feet to the rocky floor. As it was, I barely caught him in time, and we both ended up with some bruises.

I suggested scaffolding and was already reaching for my phone to call a contact, but he nixed that idea. It's too hard to move, and he needs to be able to stand back and see the whole wall sometimes. So we compromised with a cherry picker. Coordinating the teleport to get it up here was a nightmare, but the bucket is big enough to give him a few feet of workspace, plus room for extra components and tools, and I don't have to exist in a constant state of fear that he's going to injure himself. Though he has bashed his leg and hip against the side of the bucket a few times when he forgets it's there.

Speaking of things that get forgotten... "Lunchtime, Cam." It's a little early still, but between components is a good time to get his attention.

He looks around as though he'd forgotten I'm here. I'd be offended, but the way his face lights up when his gaze lands on me makes up for it. I thought things might be weird between us after my grandmother very obviously decided that if she can't matchmake him with Zac, I'll do, but he doesn't care.

Though he did ask me yesterday where we're going this weekend. So obviously he still wants a tour of Europe. We're going to France on Saturday, but we're not starting in Paris like everyone expects. Instead, I'm taking him to Les Machines de L'ile, the steampunk museum in Nantes. If I know Cam as well as I think I do, he's going to enjoy seeing those machines more than the Louvre. And when he's done there, Nantes is a nice city, has a castle, and is in a pretty part of France. It's a win all around.

"Lunch?" he asks, as though it's a new concept and not something I've been making him eat every day. "But we've only been here..." He looks at the screen of his phone and sighs. "...nearly four hours. Where does the time go?"

"You're making incredible progress," I assure him, walking over to operate the controls to bring him down. There's a panel up in the bucket, but he took one look at it and informed me there wasn't enough room in his brain to concentrate on the puzzle *and* safe machine operation. I still made sure he knows what everything is and how to use it, and there's a cheat sheet in there in case, for whatever reason, he needs to come down and I'm not able to do it, but he prefers for me to man the controls.

I don't mind. It's nice to feel useful. And I never get to play with these kinds of toys anymore, anyway.

Once he's safely on the ground, he braces his hands on my shoulders and leaps into my arms, wrapping his legs around my waist and nearly sending us both toppling to the ground. "Whoa!" I struggle to regain my balance, wrapping my arms around him protectively.

"Sorry." He pulls a meek face. "I just missed you."

I laugh. I never laughed so much before I met Cam. "You forgot I was here." But I steal a kiss anyway. I'm not ready to put him down yet, and not just because having him pressed against me makes the cave seem a bit warmer.

He gasps indignantly. "I never forget you're here. I just... zone out. Blowjob?"

In a remarkably Pavlovian response, my cock gets hard just hearing the word. Hopefully there are enough layers of down parka between us that he doesn't feel it, because I want him to eat first. He's too good at distracting me.

"After lunch."

He pouts. "But you're all the protein I need."

I back him up against the side of the truck and kiss him until my lungs feel like they'll burst from insufficient air. We break apart panting.

"So...," he gasps. "Blowjob?"

I can't say no.

His face lights up in delight, and he wriggles free of my hold and turns us around so I'm the one leaning against the truck. "Don't worry about a thing. It's my turn to take good care of you." He drops to his knees.

The cold air in the cave bites at my bare flesh as Cam frees me from my clothing, but my cock doesn't have time to wilt, because Cam's hot mouth is closing around it, taking it as deep as he can. My head falls back against the truck with a *thunk*, but I barely notice. The only thing I care about right now is Cam, his lips stretched around my dick, the wet suction of his tongue against my sensitive flesh, the way he keeps his eyes on me, a secret gleam in his gaze as he watches me slowly unravel.

He draws back, exposing my wet cock to the chill, then sucks me back into the welcome heat again. I shiver and give myself over to the magic of his mouth as he does it again, and again... and again...

Then he pulls off completely and grins up at me. "Having fun?"

My breath escapes in a huff. It's the closest I can get to a laugh with every nerve stretched to breaking point. "Brat. My dick is getting cold."

"Oh no." He widens his eyes. "Poor baby. Let me warm you up again."

I tingle in eager anticipation as he leans closer, then groan in exasperated frustration when he merely lays a light kiss on the tip, then peers up at me. "Did that help?"

The cheeky quirk of his mouth fills me with warmth. I might be desperate to come right now, but I love that he's happy and comfortable teasing me. His playful side delights me.

"I think I might need a little more," I say gravely, nudging his chin with my cock. I'm impressed with how hard it still is in the cold—testament to how fucking sexy Cam is and how much I want him.

"Hmm," he murmurs. "Let's try again." He captures the tip between his full, puffy lips, forming a tight suction grip that tears a guttural sound from me, then draws back again. "Like that?"

I manage a nod.

Taking pity on me, he slowly slides forward until his nose touches my pubic bone and the tip of my dick is in his throat. The heat, the sensation, the sight of him like that, full of me, watery eyes gazing up at me with affection and pleasure, is all it takes.

My orgasm rushes through me with all the force of a freight train.

By the time I manage to pry my eyes open, Cam's tucked me back into my pants and is standing, his front pressed to mine from shoulder to knee. "Hi."

A lazy smile curls my lips. "Hello. Fancy seeing you here."

He laughs. "I'm ready for lunch now. My break's already been longer than it should have. *Someone* took forever to come."

Snorting, I take his hand and lead him over to the table and two camp chairs. Our sandwiches and chips are in a bag there. "Yeah, that was completely *my* fault."

Throwing himself into the camp chair—which would have gone over backward if I wasn't used to him doing this and prepared to steady it—he waves off my excuse. "But you feel so good in my mouth. I wasn't giving that up sooner than I had to."

I can't see the sense in arguing with that, so I shrug and hand him his lunch. Oh no, poor me, my... person I'm having sex with likes to give playful blowjobs. How will I cope?

We talk while we eat. I spend all day with Cam, most

nights too, but we never seem to run out of things to talk about. He updates me on his progress this morning, and I look over at the wall.

"That design is incredible." I didn't see it before—I don't think any of us did but him. The elements all just looked like a jumble of metal sticking out. But now, with the two layers of components being built on, I can see it. Not a pattern, like Cam first said, though he still calls it that, insisting it is. Maybe to a puzzle designer that makes sense, but I can't tell where it will go next. All I can see is that the starting point is a giant eye, and the rest of what Cam's solved so far is a head.

A dragon head.

He's working his way down the neck at the moment. At least, that's what he tells me. When each part is complete, something about the way the components are positioned and the light hits them makes it obvious what I'm seeing, but when the components are still not perfectly in place, they're just pieces of metal. It's so fascinating. Cam's list of questions about the designer is getting longer every day.

"I wonder if it's a self-portrait," he says now. "Did the dragons who are coming know the designer personally? Would they recognize the face?"

I shrug and tip the chip packet over my mouth to catch the last few crumbs. "I don't know. The wing leader, Brandt, came last time, and he knew her. Or he said he did. He recognized her magic, anyway. But I don't know if he's coming this time." Garrett said there are four dragons coming. Two will be here for only a few hours. One will stay for a few days— apparently he's some kind of historian or archivist and wants to see everything before the door is opened. And the last one is our official dragon liaison, who will be with us for the duration.

"And they're coming on Sunday?" he asks for the millionth time. I smile indulgently at his excitement.

"Sunday," I confirm. "I checked again with Garrett this morning." Just so I could assure him of that. I think Garrett's ready to murder me if I ask him again.

"Tell me again the place we're going tomorrow?" His voice is all innocence, but I'm ready for his sneakiness.

"No. It's a surprise."

## CHAPTER EIGHTEEN

### Cam

I stare with my mouth agape at the fucking mechanical elephant crossing the courtyard in front of me. It's huge— waaaaay bigger than a real elephant—made of metal and wood, and there are people standing on a platform on its back. And it's walking.

Not willing to take my eyes off it, I grope for Micah's hand and yank him close. "There are people in it."

"Yes." He sounds like he's going to laugh. "I already bought our tickets. We can ride inside and see the gears working. I believe it also—" The elephant blows steam out of its trunk, making me jump. "—does that."

"This is the best surprise I've ever had in my life." The basic principle behind the elephant is simple, but on that scale, to safely operate it and have it work consistently... it's amazing.

Micah squeezes my hand. "There's more inside. A spider that shoots web, and I think butterflies and birds. A whole lot of animals and plants. We can also visit the workshops."

I watch the elephant return into the fancy-shed building

and finally look up at Micah. Even I can see the smug expression on his face. "The best surprise ever," I repeat.

"We're lucky." He tries to sound self-deprecating. "It's school holidays for the children right now, so they're open most of the day. Usually in winter they have very limited hours or are closed."

I make a rude noise. "Stop it. We both know this isn't what Damaris had in mind when she said you should show me Europe, but it's *exactly* what I'd love. Nobody else would have thought of bringing me here, limited hours or not."

He leans down to kiss me. "Thank me later. We have some mechanical animals to see."

We follow the elephant to the long gallery, and Micah collects a bunch of pamphlets and maps and I don't know what else.

"What first?" he asks. "The spider? Or there's a heron... it flies."

"The heron." How does he even need to ask? It *flies*.

What follows is the most fun I've ever had outside of working on a puzzle or fucking. And the latter is pretty close to being a tie. I get to work the controls of a lot of the machines, plus the machinists are there to answer any questions we have. And I have a lot. I don't speak French, but Micah does, and he patiently translates every word. The machinists don't get annoyed or bored, either—they're happy to go through everything with me.

We spend hours going through the whole gallery, ride the freaking elephant, and then visit the workshops and see the machinists working on the designs and builds. It's magical.

I let out a happy sigh as we leave the last workshop. "This has been perfect."

"We're not done yet," Micah says. I push my hair out of my eyes and look up at him.

"We're not?"

He nods toward the carousel in the square out front of the gallery. "Did you get a close look before?"

I didn't. The elephant had my attention, and I figured it was just a carousel, right? Even if, now that I look at it, it does seem a lot taller than any other carousel I've ever seen. I glance back at Micah. "I'm going to love this, aren't I?"

He shrugs, takes my hand, and leads me toward it. "Only if you love three levels of mechanical sea creatures."

It's official. I have to find a way to keep Micah.

ᛗ

I'm still considering my options when we get home late Saturday night. Micah took me to the best place for dinner—a tiny little restaurant in a building that, from the outside, looked like it might fall apart any second. Inside, though, was cozy and... okay, the candlelight helped hide the fact that the plaster was crumbling. It was even smaller than I thought, with only four two-seater tables in the whole place. It's owned by this older couple who run it with just the two of them—he's the cook and dishwasher, and she manages front of house—and the menu changes every night based on what's available at the market and what Remy feels like making. The service was half-hearted, the food divine, and I adored the whole experience. I'm definitely making Micah bring me back here.

He asked me if I wanted to stay in Nantes for the night, or anywhere in France, but I'd rather be in our bed. I've had enough new things for one day, and I need to plan.

"You're quiet," he says as we leave the teleport room. "Everything okay?"

I smile at him. "Yup. I've had the best day. I'm just tired now." And thinking. How am I going to convince Micah that we need to be together for the rest of our lives? I have just over a month before I need to be back at work, which means moving my workshop up here before then. If the puzzle keeps going at this rate, I'll have it solved in another three or four weeks, which gives me that long to make Micah realize that Team MiCam is the way to go. Then he and his cousins can help me move, and voilà! I'll be settled in and working right on schedule, just in a new place. I'll even be a *benefit* to the town. I'm an example of a non-demon who can happily live here, cut off from the world by winter and blah whatever. Plus, when Garrett turns the cave into a learning experience and tourist attraction, I can demonstrate the puzzle for visitors.

But how to pull it off?

"Are you ready for bed, or do you want—"

"Bed." Definitely bed. I want to sex him into a coma. "Naked bed."

His brow quirks. "Naked bed. I'm not going to say no."

I step right up to him and stroke his cock through his pants. "Say yes."

"Yesss."

"Are you sure?" I tease, and he plants his hands on my ass and scoops me up against his body... every hard inch of it.

"I want you to fuck me tonight," he murmurs against my lips, and excitement thrills through me. We haven't done that yet, but I want to.

"Are you sure?" I repeat, not teasing this time.

"So sure."

I pull back a little to study his face. He stares back at me, steady and confident, with a little gleam of something— excitement?—in his eyes.

"Race you to the bedroom," I declare, wiggling free of his arms and taking off down the hall. I'd half thought we could fuck in the hallway, but not for his first time bottoming. We need lots of space and a mattress. Not to mention lube—he probably won't be able to relax as easily as I can. I could enthrall him and make the need for prep redundant, but why deny him that part of the experience? Preparation can be foreplay when done right.

I hear his heavier footsteps behind me, and he snatches me into his arms three steps before I reach the bed. "Does this mean I win?" he asks.

"Cheat! You're disqualified and I'm the win—Eee!" I squeal with laughter as he tosses me onto the bed. Rolling onto my back, I grin up at him, full of my newly discovered love. He's perfect. "Get naked," I order. He blows me a kiss and pulls his sweater over his head, and I scramble to do the same. My legs get tangled in my jeans, and I kick wildly until they finally come off. When I look up, he's standing there, fully naked, arms crossed over his chest, a demon-tiny smile on his lips.

"What?"

"Just admiring your grace and coordination."

Snorting, I grab his hand and yank him onto the bed with me. "I'll show you coordination." I push him onto his back and swing my leg over his body to straddle his hips. "See?"

He laughs, and while he's distracted, I lean down and bite his left pec. Then the right one. "Yummy."

"I thought you were an incubus, not a vampire."

"Biting is for everyone," I inform him solemnly. "Want me to kiss it better?"

Micah's nod is equally solemn, and I lavish kisses across his whole chest, pausing to lick and suck his nipples. He's squirming before long, his hips moving restlessly under me, pushing his cock against my taint. The delightful surge of energy his desire gives me makes me want to draw this out forever.

"Patience," I whisper, and I'm rewarded by his growl. Okay, maybe it's time to move on.

I straighten and grab the lube from the nightstand, then kiss my way down Micah's torso until I'm face-to-dick. There's a big drop of precum at the tip, and I lick it off. "Your whole body is a delicious feast," I tell him. I'm not sure if the choked sound he makes in response is agreement or not. "Knees up," I order, and he obeys, adjusting the angle of his hips and giving me access to his ass. The angle would be easier if he was on his hands and knees, but Micah's a sensitive soul, and I think his first time bottoming will be better for him with face-to-face connection. It'll give him something to focus on.

Speaking of... I wet my fingers with lube, but before I touch Micah's ass, I lower my head and wrap my lips around his cock.

He gasps. "Your mouth is a miracle."

Aw. I give him an extra little suck as a reward, and as soon as I'm sure he's distracted, I probe delicately at his pucker. The muscle tightens reflexively, then eases enough for the tip of my finger to slip in. Micah's breathing gets a little rougher, and I tongue the underside of his dick, letting him adjust to my finger in his ass. He doesn't relax, exactly, though I wouldn't expect him to with my mouth on him, but he's not squeezing around me anymore. I slide in deeper, then shift my finger slightly—

"Ungh! Cam!"

Found it. If my mouth weren't full of cock, I'd smile smugly. I draw back a little to suckle at the head of his dick while I ease a second finger in. Micah's knees fall fully open, giving me all the room I need. He's definitely versatile—in my experience, dedicated tops don't usually like ass play this much. The pleasure he's feeling is swamping my incubus senses.

By the time I'm confident he's loose enough to take my cock, Micah's a sweaty, writhing mess, and my own dick is hard enough to pound nails. I pull my fingers out and sit back on my heels. My beautiful demon stares up at me with glazed eyes, panting. "Ready?" I ask, and he whimpers, reaching for me.

For a few seconds, I lose myself in kisses, until he whispers, "Fuck me, Cam. Please."

Lust shoots through me. Oh yeah. It's time.

I nudge the head of my cock against his hole and wait until all his attention is on me, then press forward slowly, letting him feel every millimeter of penetration. He moans, and when the ring of muscle relaxes around the narrower waist of my incubus dick, I reach out with my power and enthrall him.

Then I thrust fully into his ass, letting him feel my penetration all over again, from my perspective as well as his. He cries out, and my head falls back as the barrage of sensation increases, his pleasure rolling over me in waves. I can barely think for the intensity of it—I've never felt this before, and I'm barely holding back from orgasm after just a single thrust.

But I want to give him more.

So I pull almost all the way out, drawing an almost-sob from him, then plunge back in, setting up a steady, fast rhythm that should make his head spin.

Less than a minute later, he comes, his ass clenching around me so tightly I'm convinced I'll become part of him. I wait just long enough to imprint the ecstasy on his face into my brain, and then let go.

When I can breathe again, I lift my head from its resting place on Micah's chest and peer at his face. "Micah?"

He opens his eyes, then does a half sit-up to meet my lips in a kiss. The movement shifts me inside him, and we groan into each other's mouths.

"That was incredible," he pants.

I break away and smile. "For me, too."

Micah collapses back onto the mattress, and I carefully withdraw my cock from his ass, then join him. He wraps his arm around me and pulls me into the warmth of his side. In a minute, I'll clean us up. But right now, I'm going to bask in this moment.

𝔐

I wait until Micah's breathing evens out and his body is slack beside mine, then creep out of bed. It's a little cooler now, with the heating turned down for sleep, so I grab his shirt to wear and make for the living room, where the throw blanket on the couch will chase away the chill.

Once I'm settled in, I dial the one person I know I can rely on to come up with a plan.

"Hello, Cam! I was sure I'd hear from you sooner. How's things in the frozen mountains?"

"It's not that cold," I lie, even as I tuck the blanket more securely around myself. "Alistair, I need help."

I can almost feel him switching gears through the phone line. "Are you hurt?" His voice is no longer genial, and I realize I might have chosen my words poorly.

"No, no. That's not it. I'm fine, I promise," I race to assure him. I've only seen Alistair in super-serious mode once, and while I'll always be grateful for what he did for me then, I don't really want to see it ever again. "I need help with a plan."

"Oh, well, then you've come to the right man. I'm the king of plans. The emperor of plots. Let me just go somewhere private so I can talk freely without nosy demons listening."

Someone says something in the background, but I'm too busy remembering something I was told to listen. "Wait, Alistair—don't you work with Micah's cousin?"

"Who's Micah?"

"My cousin," that voice in the background says. "Who are you talking to?"

"I thought you said you weren't nosy and you weren't listening, Gideon?" Alistair taunts. "Lying nosy demon."

I roll my eyes. "Stop tormenting him," I order. "He might be able to help us. Can he keep a secret?" I'm sure he can, since he works for CSG, but the question is, will he keep *my* secret?

Alistair hesitates. "What's going on here, Cam?"

"I'm in love with Micah and have three weeks to show him he loves me too so we can live happily ever after."

"Mmm," Alistair replies. "I'm going to need my bros for this, Cam. Give me fifteen minutes to set up in a meeting room, and I'll call back."

"You do know you're supposed to be working?" Micah's cousin says.

"Hush, Gideon. This is of the highest importance. Clear your schedule for Operation: True Love."

"What?" Gideon and I say it at the same time.

"Fifteen minutes, Cam" is all Alistair says before the line goes dead. I pull my phone away from my ear and blink at it a few times. I guess I'm waiting fifteen minutes.

I pass the time watching YouTube videos and coming up with reasons why Alistair and Gideon, who work directly for the lucifer, would be at work on a Saturday afternoon. Not many of those reasons are good.

When the phone rings in my hand, I answer it fast. I forgot to put it on silent mode, and I don't want to wake Micah. "Alistair?"

"Never fear, Cam, the whole team is here!"

"Great!" I pause. "What team?"

"Me, Caolan, Andrew, and Gideon."

"This is stupid," a voice I recognize from before says. "I'm leaving."

"Remember what I said." Even I can hear the threat in Alistair's voice. I don't want to know what he said that makes Gideon grumble and stay.

"Thanks for coming?" I have no idea who any of the others are, but I guess Alistair thinks they can help.

"It's a true love plot!" someone says. I don't recognize the accent. "I'm thrilled to be included."

"That's Caolan," Alistair tells me. At least, I assume he's telling me. "Right, Cam. Tell us what we need to know."

I flounder a little. "I love Micah and want to live with him forever."

"Didn't you just meet him two weeks ago?" Gideon asks.

"What does time matter when love's involved?" Alistair declares dramatically. "How dare you try to keep them from each other!"

"It was only a question."

"The question was just an excuse for you to share your unsupportive—"

"Let's get back on track," another voice interrupts. This one has a French accent—I know, because I spent the whole day listening to French people.

"Micah took me to Les Machines de L'ile today," I tell them all.

There's a pause while they try to process that. "What's that?" Alistair asks.

I explain, then tell them about dinner, and the cherry picker he got for me even though all the people who had to help bitched about it. I tell them about all the times he stops me from bumping into things, and how he makes sure I eat properly and remembers what foods I like, and the way he looks at me like he's smiling on the inside. "He likes me," I finish. "I don't annoy him, and he enjoys spending time with me. I would do anything for him."

"You have to marry him," Caolan breathes. "In a ceremony under the cherry blossoms."

"There aren't any cherry trees in Hortplatz," Gideon points out.

"So they can get married somewhere else. Just think how romantic it would be."

"We can plan the wedding later," the French guy—who, by the process of elimination, must be Andrew—says. "I agree that things between you are going in the right direction. Have you talked to him about your feelings?"

*Talked to him?* My jaw drops in horror, and I sputter.

"Shh, it's okay," Alistair soothes. "He doesn't know what he's talking about. You don't have to talk to Micah about your feelings. Honestly, Andrew, what's wrong with you? Of all the stupid suggestions. I told Cam my bros would *help*, not say dumb things."

"It would resolve the situation," Gideon starts, but Alistair drowns him out.

"That's *it*! Gideon will talk to Micah."

"What?" I ask.

"What the fuck?" Gideon says.

"It's perfect. You can sound him out, see where his feelings are. We need reconnaissance. Once you have the intel, we can meet again and make a proper plan."

"I'm not talking to Micah about his feelings." Gideon sounds appalled. "We don't do that. It's bad enough I had to talk to Asher about his last month."

"You talked to Asher about his feelings?" Andrew demands. "Why is this the first I'm hearing of it? Gideon the relationship counselor." His laughter is barely contained.

Gideon's growl vibrates through the phone. "Don't make me hurt you."

"Hurt each other on your own time," Alistair says sternly. "Are we clear on the plan? Gideon's going to talk to Micah, and then we'll reassess. Be subtle, Gideon, or I'll have to have a conversation with Sam."

"I hate you."

"One more thing," Caolan interjects. "I don't want to be rude, but..."

I wait with bated breath.

"...does Gideon's grandmother like you? Because I have a good life here, and I don't want to get on her bad side."

There's an impatient huff. "My grandmother would never hurt someone Micah loved."

"But she'd come after the rest of us," Andrew adds. "Me first, probably."

"It's fine," I break in, not wanting to lose my support squad. "She likes me. She tried to set me up with Zac, but then I told her Micah and I were fucking, and she switched to him instead. She's on our side."

There's a moment of silence, and then Gideon says, "Won't someone please kill me?"

# CHAPTER NINETEEN

## Micah

Something is going on with Cam. He's been odd since we got up this morning. No... maybe since yesterday. He was quiet at dinner, even though I could tell he enjoyed himself. But it's more noticeable this morning. He's antsy, jumps anytime either of our phones makes noise, and has looked at the clock about thirty times.

"Is something wrong?" I ask finally.

His eyes go wide, and he shakes his head frantically, sending his curls flying. "No. Nothing's wrong. Why would anything be wrong?"

Uh-huh.

"You seem a little... out of sorts."

"Nope. Why would you think that? I'm excited! Yep, excited. The dragons are coming today!"

That's true. He's been looking forward to this all week. Maybe he's nervous. Most people don't get the chance to meet an actual dragon, much less four of them. And they'll be examining his work... sort of. If any of them dares say something to upset him, I'll make sure they regret it, but I can understand why the anticipation might be getting to him.

He needs a distraction. "Why don't I call Asher and see if he and Garrett want to go to the pub for lunch?" I suggest. It's early still, but we can also walk out to the snow village and see the progress Zoe's made. Last weekend, she had miniature snow people skating on a little snow pond. We had a few substantial snowfalls this week, so she's had a lot of material to work with.

"No!"

I freeze mid-reach for my phone. What's going on with him?

He must see my surprise, because he hastens to add, "I mean, yes, that sounds like fun, but I'll call Garrett. You leave your phone free." He dashes off before I can ask what that's supposed to mean. Leave my phone free? For what?

I can hear his voice in the other room, so he's clearly making the call. Whatever it is that's worrying him, I hope it stops soon. Or he tells me so I can help him.

Could it be the snow? The lack of diversity in the village? The lack of shops and nightlife? He didn't seem interested in any of that before, and it's only been two weeks... but maybe being in a city yesterday reminded him that he prefers that kind of environment. Maybe he was so desperate to be the one to call Garrett because he wants to talk to him privately, ask for advice on how to cope.

I know he's not asking if he can leave. There's no way he'd ever leave the puzzle wall unfinished. I'm counting on that— it gives me a few more weeks with him, at least, to build our relationship. By then he'll hopefully be open to something long-distance between us, with me visiting every weekend. And then maybe just staying with him for most of the week. And then moving in with him. I'll miss living here, but I can still visit often and see my family. It's more important that Cam is comfortable and happy.

I finally understand why Asher was such a lovesick fool

last year. Even though I'm not completely certain that what I feel is love—too soon—I know it could easily become love, if given the chance. And knowing that, I'll happily and with gusto rip apart anyone who dares upset Cam. The thought actually makes me a little giddy. I wonder if Cam would appreciate seeing me smite his enemies?

Does he even have enemies? Maybe that one random guy who keeps texting him. I could smite him.

I'm thinking about the finer details of smiting someone—does it have to be with a sword, for instance—when my phone rings. Gideon's name is on the screen, and I answer quickly. He prefers to text rather than call.

"Gideon? Is everything okay?"

"Of course," he snaps. "Can't I just call you?"

Ahh, there's our murder baby. He's always been this grumpy, even before he knew what the word meant. I have fond memories of him scowling at us from his perambulator.

"It's always good to hear from you. How's Sam?" I met his longtime boyfriend—and the head of the community of species—in person for the first time last summer. We've managed to catch up a few times since then, including at Asher's wedding. "Has he pulled any more muscles dancing?"

"We don't speak of that," Gideon warns. He's rabidly protective of Sam. Murder baby has a favorite toy. "He's good. Busy with work. Why are people such asshats?"

I lean back in my chair and put my feet on the coffee table. "Some of them come by it naturally."

"We should be allowed to kill those people," he grumbles. "What have you been up to?"

I sit up and put my feet back on the floor. The question sounded awkward, probably because Gideon never asks stuff like that. But then, he never randomly calls, either. Is today some kind of nexus of weirdness? Should I expect Grandmother to suggest we invite her worst enemies to dinner?

"Are you sick?" I ask Gideon. "You never like to chat."

There's a moment of silence, and then he sighs. "Sam says I need to be more social. He wanted me to join a sporting team or a club or something stupid like that, so I said I'd be social with people I can tolerate."

I grin and return to my former comfortable position, feet finding their place on the table. That sounds more like Gideon. "As one of the few people you can tolerate, I'd like to thank Sam for the leverage this gives me." The growl that reverberates down the line makes me want to laugh. He's so predictable. "You need to be social, hm? You could come for a visit. We have dragons arriving this afternoon."

"I know. Who do you think had to tell Grandmother? And then argue with her over the details? I get enough dragons at work, thanks."

"Are they troublesome? Cam's excited about meeting them, but if they're going to hurt his feelings, I can run interference."

"Troublesome, yes. But they won't hurt anyone's feelings." He hesitates. "So... Cam. You sound very protective of him."

I briefly consider recording this conversation. Gideon attempting casual gossip is hilarious. He's trying, though, and since Cam is possibly talking to Garrett about how much he doesn't want to be here, it can't hurt to get another opinion, right?

"How did you know Sam was the one for you?"

The *meep* sound that comes down the line isn't one I've ever heard Gideon make before. He clears his throat. "I beg your pardon. Um. Yes. Sam."

This isn't going well. "Never min—"

"No, no. I have this. It's important." He pauses. "I don't know."

That's approximately the level of helpfulness I was expecting from him. "Okay. What about *when* did you know?"

He makes a humming sound. "Did Asher tell you I wasn't completely truthful when I told you how Sam and I met?"

"No?" I make a mental note to ask Asher about this later. How dare he have interesting information and not share it?

"We had a one-night stand."

"Ha, just like Asher," I crow. "I'll have to warn Zac to stay away from casual hookups unless he wants to end up married."

Gideon ignores me. "Then he started working for CSG. I was horrified, and I... avoided him for five years."

"Avoided him how?" I didn't miss that little pause. There's something he's not telling me.

"He claims to have thought I was going to murder him. An exaggeration, but I possibly did use some intimidation tactics to keep him from getting close."

I can see I'm going to need to ask Sam about this. Or maybe Garrett can ask his cousin Alistair. He might know, since he worked there too and is Sam's friend. "And then what? What changed?"

"He joined our team, and I started working more closely with him. We... had words and cleared the air. Soon..." He pauses again. "Soon I knew I couldn't breathe without him."

The words are uncharacteristically sentimental, and they hit me in the feelings with the force of a punch. I know what he means. Not exactly—what's between me and Cam is still growing. But I find myself constantly looking for him, checking on him. If I don't know that he's okay, it makes me anxious. He needs me, and I need him to need me.

"When..." It's my turn to pause and clear my throat. "When did he feel the same?" I don't have the luxury of seeing Cam every day for months to prove that we should take our relationship to the next level. When he goes home, can I even expect that he'll want to see me again? And if he does, how will he feel about monogamy? Maybe he'll want to see other people as well.

I'm not too worried about that, though. Seeing other people would mean leaving his house and his puzzles, and if he knows I'm ready to drop everything and be there for him at a moment's notice, he's not likely to want to be bothered going out.

Gideon sighs. "It's hard to say. I didn't want to show affection or talk about it, so I don't know if he was waiting for me to wake up or if he genuinely didn't feel anything yet. Then... something happened that I can't talk about because it's classified, and I moved him in with me after."

I squint a little as I think about that. It sounds like he didn't ask Sam to move in, which... yeah, that checks out. Gideon's always been bossy, even as the youngest of us. I can see him moving Sam into his house without asking first.

"If you have feelings for Cam, you should talk to him." He sounds uncomfortable just saying the words. "Maybe he has feelings too but is afraid to say something. You could both get old and die afraid and alone."

"Have you been talking to Grandmother?" That's one of her favorite arguments to nag us about settling down. Never mind that we're not even two hundred yet and have nearly a millennium ahead of us.

"No. I've been avoiding her since the wedding. After everything that happened, I'm afraid she might insist that I move to Hortplatz to escape all the crazy people in my life."

He does have a lot of crazy people in his life. Like Garrett's cousin, and that vampire Grandmother hates. Sam can be interesting sometimes too.

"Talking to Cam sounds smart on the surface, but what if it turns out this is just a fling for him?"

"I don't think talking to him will change that, if it's the case," Gideon points out. "If you're worried, wait until right before he's going to leave to bring it up. But I very, very strongly recommend that you talk to him about this as soon as possible. Now, even. Right now." He mutters something else that sounds like "and end my misery," but that can't be right. I must have misheard him in my distracted state.

"I suppose. The other problem is how I'm going to tell Grandmother I'm moving."

Gideon coughs. "What? Are you insane? She'll kill you just so she can keep your corpse in the village." He hesitates. "Only not in as weird a way as that sounds. Also, never tell Sam I said that. He's convinced that Grandmother hates him and wants to kill him, and this doesn't fit with me telling him she's just tough on the surface."

"Tough on the surface?" I echo incredulously. My grandmother loves me and has a good, kind heart, but she's as tough as old boots all the way through.

"He doesn't spend enough time with her to know it's not true. Why are you moving?"

I shrug, even though he can't see me. "Cam doesn't live here. And I don't think he likes it. Ever since we went to Nantes yesterday, he's been acting funny. I think seeing the city and all the amenities brought home to him how different it is here. And the cold. He doesn't like the cold much, either."

Gideon makes a sound that's half growl, half sigh. "Talk to him," he says again. "Please, for the love of my sanity. Talk to him."

"You're such a diva. Why are you being so dramatic?"

"*I'm* being dramatic? Have you heard yourself? Wah, wah, the man who barely lets me out of bed and happily spends all day, every day with me might not like me. But I can't ask because I'm *scared*."

"I don't sound like that," I protest. I don't. The words sound a little familiar, though.

"One day, I'm going to make you pay for putting me through this," he threatens.

"You're the one who called me and wanted to be social. Maybe I should send Sam a message and tell him you said you wanted to learn how to play..." I try to think of a sport that would drive Gideon bonkers. "...water polo." He's always hated swimming.

"Talk. To. Your. Lover. Fuck! That idiot Alistair has me saying stupid words now. I'm hanging up. Get off your ass and tell Cam how you feel." The call ends while I'm still trying to understand what he's talking about.

# CHAPTER TWENTY

## Cam

It's a stunning day, the sky a deep, endless blue, sunlight reflecting dazzlingly off the snow. The pub has opened its outdoor seating area, heaters and lap blankets chasing away the chill for those of us sitting there. If someone had asked me last month if I'd eat outdoors on a day this cold, I'd have thought it was a trick question. But it's actually a great experience, and the view of the mountains today is stupendous.

Too bad I'm so distracted, I can't enjoy any of that. My mind is firmly stuck on the fact that even though I *know* Micah's cousin Gideon called him before, Alistair hasn't sent me an update yet. That has to be bad news, right? If Micah had told Gideon that he was madly in love with me and designing our forever home, Alistair would have already called, right?

My phone beeps—loudly, since I turned the volume all the way up—and I jump as I fumble it out of my pocket. I had it on the table before, and Garrett asked if I was expecting a call.

"Is everything all right?" he asks now, frowning at me in concern. "You've been rather unsettled today."

"I'm fine!" I smile brightly to prove it, then look down at my screen. There's two texts from a number I don't recognize, but maybe that's just Gideon texting me directly? I tap to check.

UNKNOWN CONTACT:

theres nowhere ur safe from me

I sigh. Still with this. I might need to do as Micah keeps urging me and talk to Enforcement. I don't know whether Cary Mack is a member of the community or not, but if he's human, maybe they have some contacts with the human police who can handle it.

"Something important?" Micah asks, and I glance up to find his gaze on me. Asher and Garrett are distracted, talking to a passerby who stopped and is leaning on the railing of the pub's terrace. The sunshine and relative warmth have brought most of the village out, walking, snowshoeing, sledding, and skating. The snow village rang with children's delighted laughter when we went past earlier. And it's all hidden away up here, safe from outsiders. I can see why the demons like it.

"Not important," I assure Micah, putting my phone away.

He frowns, looking forbidding and scary, and affection rushes through me in a warm wave. My big tough demon. "It was him again, wasn't it?"

"Yes. I think you might be right about talking to Enforcement."

Garrett turns back just in time to hear that. "Enforcement? Why do you need Enforcement?"

"It's not a big deal." I explain it to him quickly. "He keeps texting me, and Micah's worried about it. So..." I shrug. "I might see if Enforcement can do anything."

Asher looks at his cousin. "If they can't, just let me know."

Nodding, Micah says, "That was my backup plan. Gideon first, then you."

I glance between the two of them, then over at Garrett, who's shaking his head in exasperation. "What?"

"He can't harass you with texts if he doesn't have enough money to buy burner phones," Asher says with a shrug. I still don't get it, and Micah must see my confusion.

"Asher knows a lot of people in the finance world. And a lot of ways to destroy someone's credit."

I gasp. "That's terrible!" But if Enforcement can't help, I won't say no. I guess that makes me a hypocrite.

Oh, well.

"Have you told Alistair about this?" Garrett asks, frowning slightly. "I wouldn't have thought he'd let you go this long without getting Enforcement involved."

I set my jaw stubbornly. "Alistair's not the boss of me. He doesn't 'let' me do anything. But no. I haven't told him." Because if I did, he'd take over and handle it all like last time. I'll always be grateful to Alistair, but I don't need him to look after me.

"Please, *please* don't bring your annoying cousin into this," Asher says to Garrett.

"I'll second that. I'm still not recovered from the last time I spoke to him," Micah adds. "In the nicest possible way, I'd be happy to never see him again."

Dread curls inside me. I can't choose between Micah and Alistair. "You're kidding, right? He's a bit exuberant, but Alistair's the best person I know." I wince when it comes out a little louder and more vehement than I intended.

"The *best* person?" Asher sounds skeptical.

"The very best." I fold my arms. If Micah has a problem with Alistair, we need to sort this out now, because Alistair will always be welcome in my home.

Garrett sighs. "As much as it pains me, I have to agree with Cam on this. Alistair is the world's biggest pain in the ass, but he's the most dependable friend anyone could have."

Micah says nothing, but he's studying my face. "If you both say so, I'll believe it. Maybe I should spend more time with him." He tries to keep his face demon-blank, but it still looks like he's sucking on a lemon. I laugh.

"Just don't write him off. He throws the best parties, anyway."

"Yes," Asher says dryly. "He had some input at our wedding."

That sounds like a story I want to hear, so I—

Shouts from down the street grab our attention. I lean over the railing and see people peering up at the sky and pointing.

So I look.

"Fuck me!" Micah's exclamation drowns out my gasp. "Dragons!"

"Dragons," I repeat reverently. There are four of them, getting closer by the second. Two are green, one red, and the last rosy pink. They're huge, even from this distance, and majestic and fucking amazing. "Every day of my life just keeps getting better since I came here."

"Did you know they were flying here?" Asher demands, and I take my eyes off the dragons for long enough to see Garrett raise a brow at him.

"Of course. How did you think they were going to get here?"

I look back at the real-life dragons approaching. Wow.

"I don't know! I thought someone was going to get them. Or that an elf would bring them through a portal."

I blink. An elf would bring them through a what now?

Before I can ask if portal means the same thing to them that it does to me, and if so, why haven't I heard anything about elves being able to use them, Garrett says, "Well, they flew. And they're here now. Are we going to go meet them?"

I'm out of my chair so fast, it nearly tips over. Then the

blanket that was in my lap tangles with my legs, and I bump into the table, rattling all our dishes. I stay on my feet, though. Score for me!

"I think Cam would like to go." There's only the tiniest trace of sarcasm in Micah's voice, and his subtle little smile more than makes up for it.

We pay the bill, promise to tell the dragons they get a discount at the pub, and make our way through town to what Garrett tells us is the designated landing area. The dragons are circling above us now.

"Here?" Asher asks, looking around. We're on the south side of the village, in an area that's relatively clear but not level. The older teens use it for sledding when they can get away with it, which isn't often, because it's too steep and too close to buildings to be safe. "Don't they need a flat area?"

Garrett shrugs. "I asked, and they said no. As long as it's not wooded, apparently." A small crowd gathers around us as the dragons begin to descend—one green one and the pink one first, while the other two continue to circle.

"Micah, Micah!" I hear Isaac calling, but don't take my eyes off the smooth way the dragons land on the uneven slope. I could never be that graceful.

Micah leaves my side but is back a moment later with Isaac in his arms and Chloe tagging along beside him. "Wow," Chloe breathes. "I can't believe those are real dragons."

"I know." I'm in complete agreement.

A gasp runs through the group of onlookers—including me—when the two dragons on the ground shift into biped form. They're both men, both dark-haired, but where one is tall, hair cut short, with a stern expression, the other couldn't be more opposite. His hair flops in his face, and he grins and waves at us jauntily.

"That's Steffen," Asher says. "He was here a few weeks ago. He's in charge of dragon security."

That cheerful guy? I guess that'll teach me not to judge a book by its cover.

"Which one?" Isaac demands. "That one, or that one?" He points.

Micah captures his hand and pulls it down. "Don't point. The taller one."

Oh. Whoops. Look at me making assumptions about making assumptions.

Garrett walks forward to meet them even as the other two dragons swoop in to land. Asher takes Chloe's hand and follows, and Micah slides a glance at me. "Well? Come on."

Yesssssss. I'm gonna meet the dragons!

It doesn't go as smoothly as I'd hoped. For one thing, this part of the village doesn't get the snow removal treatment, what with being a big, empty space. Teens hang out here enough that the lower layers have been packed down, but I still have to slog through nearly a foot of it. Plus, the ground underneath is uneven.

So of course I trip and face-plant into the snow. Micah couldn't even catch me, since he's carrying Isaac.

I groan into the cold, wet snow. Why can I never make a good first impression?

"Cam?" Hands grasp my shoulders and lift me back to my feet. "Did you hurt yourself?" Micah studies my face.

I blow snow off my lips. I shouldn't have pulled my scarf down before, but I wanted to see the dragons better. "Yes. My pride is never going to recover. Everyone saw, didn't they?"

"Not everyone," Isaac assures me solemnly. "Most of them were looking at the dragons." He tilts his head. "You look like a snow monster."

Micah coughs, but I know he's trying not to laugh. I sigh. "It could be worse," I tell Isaac. "I could have been eaten by a snow monster."

He nods. "That would be a lot worse. Do you need help brushing off the snow?" He begins vigorously patting and brushing my legs, and I grin.

"Thanks. You're such a big help."

Micah's smiling at me with warm tenderness, and I wonder if he's got a thing for snow monsters. "Help, Micah," I order, and begin beating snow off my arms and torso. He chuckles but obeys, and it's only a minute before I feel more human.

Cold. But human.

I turn back in the direction of the dragons and see the other two have also shifted to biped form, and there are now four men talking to Garrett and Ash—

"Whoa. Are those two twins?" They have to be. They're identical, except for their clothes and the fact that one has slightly longer hair.

"Looks like," Micah agrees.

"I've never met identical twins before. And now I'm going to meet identical dragon twins." I forge forward through the snow, trying to be more careful this time but not delaying.

One of the twins—the stern one, the guy who's in charge of security—sees me coming. His glare would be impressive if I wasn't surrounded by demons twenty-four seven. Frowns don't scare me anymore.

Well... not much.

# CHAPTER TWENTY-ONE

### Micah

I don't like the way that Steffen guy is frowning at Cam. I scowl right back at him, warning him with my eyes not to say anything mean.

"Oh good! Here he is," Garrett says cheerfully. "This is Camden Torrence, our puzzle expert. He's made excellent progress already. Cam, come and say hello."

Cam forges forward, and I hurry to stay within grabbing distance in case he trips again. Isaac stomps along in my wake.

"This is Steffen, Wil, Fabian, and Ronan." Garrett gestures to each dragon as he introduces them. I know Steffen from when he came to the cave with the wing leader, but the others are strangers to me.

Wil is the first one to offer Cam his hand. "It's so great to meet you. I have one of your puzzles—Alistair gave it to Steffen, who gave it to me. You've got incredible talent."

Cam's cheeks flush. "Oh. Thank you. I'm glad you like it. Wow. A dragon likes my puzzle."

"Loves your puzzle," Wil corrects. "We're on your wait list for an order too."

"Really?" Cam looks agonized, and I know what he's thinking. He wants to bump them up the list, but other people have been waiting longer.

"We're happy to wait," Wil assures him, earning my friendship. "I just wanted you to know how much of a fan I am."

Cam smiles brightly. "I'm a fan too. Of you."

"He's taken," Steffen says sharply. "I don't think his boyfriend would like—"

"Oh, no!" Cam shakes his head. "Not like that. I'm taken too. Well, I'm mostly taken for now. I just meant... dragons. Like... wow."

Steffen doesn't seem impressed, but Wil's smiling. "We can be mutual fans, then. If you have questions about dragons, you should talk to Fabian. He's our species historian."

I look at Fabian, who has floppy black hair and a cheeky smile. He's talking quietly to Chloe and Isaac, but I hear, "I don't know anyone called Ed. I can ask around, if you like."

Sighing, I make a mental note to talk to Isaac again about the fact that Ed the dragon is imaginary. Or maybe I'll get Dad to do it, so I don't have to be the bad guy.

"Ronan is going to be our expert consultant on all things dragon," Garrett says. From the looks of Ronan's face, he's deeply unhappy about this.

Cam must be thinking the same thing, because he says, "You'll love the village. I know the snow seems daunting, but trust me, everyone here will take really good care of you. Plus, you've got wings and all, so you can come and go as you please. And the cave is so exciting! I can't wait to get the door open."

If anything, Ronan's expression becomes even more tragic. He's the other twin, but they don't seem much alike apart from their looks. Of course, it's hard to tell for sure when Ronan looks like he wants to curl up and die, and Steffen looks like he wants everyone else to die.

The awkward moment is broken when Fabian says, "Brrr! It might be a sunny day, but man, it's cold! When you told us to wear winter gear, you weren't kidding."

"Let's get you inside," Garrett says instantly. "The village council wants to meet you, anyway. We'll get that done, get something hot to drink, and then I bet you want to see the cave."

"Yes!" Fabian cries emphatically, while Wil nods. Ronan says nothing.

"Has there been much progress since I was here last?" Steffen asks as we turn and start heading back toward the main part of the village. Most of the crowd has wandered off, since a bunch of men standing around talking aren't as interesting as dragons.

"I haven't been there this week," Garrett admits. "I'm trying to pace myself. Micah?"

"Lots of progress," I confirm. "I'll let Cam explain it when we get there, but he discovered that the puzzle is layered. Just wait until you see—I still can't believe it sometimes, and I see it every day."

"Puzzles are like that," Cam agrees, slipping a hand into mine. "They constantly delight and amaze."

"The puzzle Cam made me is amazing," Chloe confirms from his other side. "You have to move all the parts to solve it. He's coming to our school this week to show everyone else how they work, but Isaac and me already know because he made us some."

"Mine is hard," Isaac admits, "but Cam helped me. He's the best. My mom says Micah better keep him, or she'll start thinking he's a changeling because no child of hers would be dumb enough to let Cam go."

My brain freezes. My mother said *what?*

Garrett coughs, and when I glance over at him, his face is alight with stifled laughter. "Cam's definitely special" is all he says.

Cam, who hasn't reacted to my brother's comments in any way—maybe he thinks it's just more matchmaking?—twists around to look at Ronan. "See how nice they all are?"

"Too bad Ronan can't date Micah too," Fabian says blithely.

Wil winces. "Fabian—"

"Unless you're polyamorous? Then it could work out. Hey, Ronan, are you even into men? I just realized I don't know that about you."

"Yes." Ronan's voice is low. "But, uh... one at a time. And not other people's."

"Good," Cam declares before Fabian can say anything else. "I'm sure polyamory works for a lot of other people, but I'm a little possessive."

"What's possive mean?" Isaac asks, and I look around for my parents or any relative. Asher, the asshole, is smirking.

"*Possessive*," Cam stresses the word, "means I don't like sharing."

My brother shakes his head. "Me neither, but you should try. Sometimes people just want to play with your stuff for a little while, and then they give it back."

Asher laughs out loud, and there are a few snickers from the dragons. Garrett and Cam are the only ones who seem to be able to keep straight faces.

"Cam will have to try that out," Garrett says solemnly. "I see your dad over there. We're going to the council meeting now, so you'd better go with him."

"Okay. C'mon, Chloe." He takes off in Dad's direction, shouting over his shoulder, "Bye! It was nice meeting you!"

"I can't wait until Cecylia is that age. Do you think she'll be that cute?" Fabian asks. "Maybe Rhys and I should start planning to have a fledgling."

"Really?" Wil asks, even as Steffen's eyes widen in alarm. "You lost your socks four times last week."

Fabian blinks at him. "So?"

"So do you really think you're ready for a fledgling?"

With a confused frown, Fabian says, "Fledglings aren't socks."

"No, I know that. What I mean is—"

"Ooh, how cute are fledgling socks? Cecylia's are so tiny!"

I actually see the moment Wil gives up. "Is Cecylia your child?" I ask him.

He shakes his head. "No, she's Brandt's. And Percy's—the former lucifer?"

"Really?" I didn't know the previous lucifer had a child. Gideon did mention that he was now in a relationship with Brandt, the dragon wing leader, but nothing about a baby. "Garrett, did you know that?"

"Yes. Alistair asked me for help choosing a present when the baby was born. He wanted to know what the perfect gift would be for the child of two leaders from different species who bridged a dimensional gap. I sent him a link to the newborn page of a local toy store, and he called me a killjoy."

"That sounds like Alistair," Wil murmurs as we turn onto the street where the post office and council building is. "This village is charming. It's cold here, but pretty."

"I first arrived in the late summer, and it's beautiful then," Garrett says. "How did you find the conditions flying in? Do you think other dragons might enjoy visiting here?"

"The flight was awesome." Fabian's gaze goes dreamy. "So many updrafts on a day like this. Lots of fun."

That reminds me... "I don't want to be rude, but is there any chance humans saw you fly overhead?"

The look Steffen gives me is approving. "No," he replies.

"We used a distortion shield coded to only allow members of the community to see us."

I'm not sure exactly what a distortion shield is, but I'm going to guess it makes them invisible. "I like the sound of that magic."

Cam snorts. "You're the social one," he reminds me. "You *like* people."

Smiling at him, I reply, "I like *our* people. Humans, not so much."

"Some humans are nice," he protests. "My neighbors are great."

"Your neighbors, the crime kingpins?"

"Don't be judgy. They've been perfectly nice to me."

I make an agreeing sound, but when I meet Steffen's gaze, I shake my head. His mouth sets in a line, and he nods. I'm not sure what that means, but we're bonding. It can't be a bad thing to have a dragon on my side.

We stop in front of the post office. "This won't take long," Garrett promises again. "Why don't you three get everything ready to go to the cave? Find Zac if you can—it will take less time to get there if there are three of you teleporting. We can go in one trip."

I lean toward Asher. "Your hellhound is bossy."

Garrett gives me a death stare. I'm fairly sure that if he wasn't trying to be professional and impress the dragons, he'd be flipping me off.

"I'll find Zac," I promise.

Cam gives a jaunty wave as I adjust my grip on his hand. "See you soon!"

I teleport us back to the house I share with my cousins and hustle Cam out of the teleport room so Asher can follow. "Zac?" I call.

"Za-ac," Cam echoes, leading the way to the kitchen. I

redirect him just before his shoulder makes contact with the doorframe, and he smiles at me over his shoulder. "Thanks."

Zac looks up from the crumbs of his lunch. He has papers spread out over the table and doesn't seem all that pleased to see us. "You're back early. Didn't the dragons like the cave?"

"We haven't been yet," Cam says, planting himself in one of the chairs while I head for the coffee maker. "Did you hear the fuss when they arrived? Why didn't you come out to meet them?"

He shrugs. "I wanted to read this, and then I got an idea for a safe way to ski on that slope behind the village. I can meet the dragons later, right?"

"No," I tell him. "Garrett's volunteered you to teleport some of them to the cave."

He rolls his eyes. "Fine. Where are they?"

"Meeting the village council." Cam's picked up a sheet of paper from the table. "Micah, you should look at this. I think it could work."

"It's just a sketch," Zac starts, but I take the sheet and scan over it. Zac's got a good understanding of how mountains work, so it's not surprising that he's considered most of the risk factors people usually overlook when planning something like a ski resort.

"This could definitely work." I'd want to see a land survey first, of course, but it looks possible. "I didn't know you were thinking about this."

My cousin shrugs. "It was never feasible, with us being cut off all winter. There are more accessible places to ski. Even we don't really ski around here, with it being so risky."

"But now that Garrett's looking into ways to get people here during winter..."

"It's an option we might want to consider."

"What's an option we might want to consider?" Asher

asks, coming into the kitchen and stealing the coffee mug from my hand. Family is such a burden.

"Nice beard burn" is all I say. Complaining about the theft would just make him happy.

"Don't be jealous because my sexy husband wants me." He nods toward the paper in my hand. "What's that?"

"Zac's got an idea for a ski resort," Cam enthuses. "What a perfect way to bring more people to the village! I've never skied before."

My head throbs lightly at the thought of the harm Cam could come to—and cause—on skis. "I'll teach you." The words are out before I can stop them, and I can't regret them when they made him smile so big.

"Really? I'm not too clumsy?"

I hesitate. "You might fall a few times." Or a few hundred. Hopefully he'll be so sick of getting his ass wet, he'll give up before we have to leave the bunny slope. If we have a bunny slope. The area's not really bunny-slope-friendly.

His beautiful brown eyes are all soft and trusting as he gazes up at me. "That's okay. You'll help me up."

No matter what, there will be a bunny slope.

# CHAPTER TWENTY-TWO

## Cam

"It'll be a few years before it's up and running," Zac says, smashing my tender moment with Micah. "Does that mean you'll be back to visit us, Cam?"

Okay, I can forgive him for butting in, since he's just given me the perfect opening to say how much I like it here. "Oh, for sure! The cave is here, and Garrett says the village is gorgeous in summer. I have to see that. Plus, I have friends here now... right?" Suddenly, I'm not so confident. What if they're all impatiently waiting for me to leave so they never have to see me again?

"Chloe and Isaac would cry if you never came back," Asher informs me. Then he grins wickedly, big enough that I have no problem seeing it. "Zac, did you hear about what Isaac said today?"

"Asher," Micah warns. Asher ignores him.

"Apparently Aunt Hilda likes Cam so much, she thinks no child of hers could be stupid enough to let him go."

Oh yeah. I'd nearly forgotten that. Good to know Hilda is on my side. I should mention that to Alistair when he calls.

If he ever calls. We're going to the cave soon, and there's no signal up there. What if I miss his call?

"Cam is pretty great," Zac's saying, a teasing glint in his eye. "But I'm not sure Micah's that smart. Has Aunt considered a DNA test?"

"I hate you both," Micah says flatly, then turns to me. "Ignore them. They're children."

Ignore them? What does that mean? That he doesn't want to keep me and considers that the intelligent decision?

This no longer seems like a positive thing. I need Micah thinking of how well I fit in with his family, not that the idea of me staying is childish.

Before I can think of a response, Asher claps his hands. "Garrett said to be waiting. Let's go."

Zac shakes his head incredulously. "Did you just clap your hands like we're babies?"

"Act like babies, be treated like babies. Also, Garrett does it and I've picked up the habit. Come on. We don't want to piss him off again."

"Do we need any gear?" Zac stands and goes to grab his coat off the hook by the back door.

"No, everything's still in the cave." Micah's watching me, his expression back to demon-blank. I wish I knew what he was thinking. He holds a hand out to me as Zac rejoins us, buttoning his coat, and I take it.

The familiar whirl of teleporting is welcome. It gives me a valuable second away from Micah's gaze. What am I going to do now?

The teleport room at the post office is exactly as I remember it—boring. We step out so Zac and Asher can follow, and we're just in time to see the door to the council meeting room open.

"...show them the cave, and then go from there," Garrett is saying. He steps into the hall, sees us, and mouths, "Help."

Damaris's voice carries out to us. "I really think it would be more comfortable for Ronan and Fabian to stay with me."

"What now?" Asher murmurs from behind us, and I look over my shoulder.

"We didn't hear it all, but Garrett wants help."

Sighing, he ducks around us and strides forward. Garrett is still loitering right outside the meeting room door, and I can see half of Wil too.

"Sorry to interrupt, but we need to get going," Asher calls. "Ready?"

"No." Damaris is standing firm. "We haven't decided where our guests are staying."

"We set up a house for them," Asher tells her. "Remember? The pantry is stocked and everything."

"That's not very homey or welcoming, though."

"What's she up to?" Zac whispers. "She doesn't ever invite strangers to stay with her."

"Grandmother," Asher begins, a note of strained patience in his voice. "I'm about ninety percent certain that we can make our guests feel welcome and at home while also allowing them the privacy of their own accommodations. What if they came to family dinner tonight?"

There's a moment of frigid silence, during which we all know Asher is now on Damaris's shit list. "Very well. If you think that's the best path. I would hate to make anyone feel bulldozed or uncomfortable."

I wince. "Poor Asher," I whisper to Micah, who shrugs.

"He'll survive. She still loves him for marrying Garrett."

Garrett and Asher manage to extricate all the dragons and firmly close the door, then hustle them toward us. "This is Zac," Garrett introduces. "Have any of you ever been teleported before?"

Three heads shake, but Fabian nods enthusiastically. "Sure! There was this demon, and—"

"Just a yes is enough, Fabian," Wil interrupts. "Especially if this is from before you met Rhys. Nobody needs to hear about your sex life."

"Yes." Fabian nods again. "I've been teleported."

"Did you feel sick after? I'm not sure if teleport sickness affects dragons," Garrett frets.

"I was a little nauseous, but that could also have been because of the... uh. Because of other stuff we were doing."

I'm so curious now. I make a mental note to ask Fabian about it when Wil's not around.

"So you might feel a tad unwell," Garrett warns. "One of my delightful demon in-laws will take hold of your shoulder or arm or something, and a moment after that, we'll be in the cave."

Steffen frowns. "Why can't we fly up there?"

"You can if you'd like to, but we don't have any markers outside the cave. So you'd need to wait until we get up there and can wave at you."

"This would be faster," Wil says. He's looking at Steffen. "You're in charge."

Steffen's still frowning fiercely, but he finally nods. "I'll go first."

"We can all go at the sam—" Garret begins, but Micah interrupts.

"You're with me, then. We'll go ahead and get the lights on." He wraps an arm around my shoulders and holds out his other hand to Steffen, who hesitates, then steps forward to take it. "Ready?"

Steffen nods, and the world falls away.

The darkness of the cave is familiar, as is the flash of Micah's cell phone as he turns on the flashlight and gropes for the lights. When they come on, Steffen rises out of his half-crouch. I'm not sure what he was doing, but it kind of looked defensive. Did he think we were going to attack him?

"Let's move over this way," I suggest, "and leave a clear space for the others."

He obliges, turning his attention to the rest of the cave, scanning it from end to end. Only then does he look at the wall—and gasp. "That's not what I was expecting at all."

"It surprised all of us," I say happily. "C'mon, and I'll explain."

"Wait for the others," Micah calls, even as they appear. Fabian is talking, literally midsentence, and Wil is looking around even before he gets his legs under himself, but Ronan moans and stumbles to his knees.

"What's wrong?" Steffen snaps, striding in his direction. "Are you hurt?"

"I'm dying," Ronan groans.

"Teleport sickness," Zac explains, looking down at him. "Just keep breathing steadily, and it will pass."

I wince. It seems Zac's not the best person to have around when you're not feeling well.

"I wish you'd fucking pass," Ronan hisses, then moans again.

"I'll get you some water," I offer hastily. "Zac, come with me."

He blinks in confusion as Steffen kneels beside his brother. "What? Why do you—"

"Now, Zac," Garrett orders. Zac shakes his head but joins me in the equipment corner. There's a cooler here with bottled water in it—Micah keeps it stocked for us. Ironically, the cooler is to keep it from getting too cold. The temperature in the cave drops well below freezing overnight, and we don't need bottled ice.

"Did nobody ever tell you sick people like sympathy?" I whisper to him as I open the cooler.

He shrugs. "Sympathy isn't going to help him feel better. Breathing steadily will."

Before I can explain to him all the ways he's wrong, Garrett joins us, glaring at Zac. "Are you trying to make this go badly? Do you hate me? Is that what this is?"

"Uh... what?"

"Be nice to the dragons, Zac. Be *nice*. Do you know what nice means?"

"I'm being nice!" he protests. I decide to leave them to it and take the water to Ronan. Garrett seems to have the conversation under control.

Micah's brought over a chair, and Steffen's helping Ronan into it when I arrive. He's pale and looks shaky, but hasn't thrown up, which I'm told is a good sign.

"Here, sip this." I hand him the water. "I'm sorry you were affected so badly." I mean... it's not my fault, but it seems like the thing to say.

"Why am I the only one?" He takes the bottle, opens it, and sips. Then freezes. We all wait with bated breath to see if the water is going to come back up.

It doesn't.

"I was a little dizzy," Wil says. "It affects everyone differently, right?"

"That's right," Micah confirms. "Cam doesn't get sick at all, but my cousin Gideon's boyfriend is affected like Ronan. He used to vomit, too."

Ronan gags. "Could we not talk about... that?"

"Sorry." Micah winces. "It does usually get better over time, though. The more often you're teleported, the more used to it your body will get."

The appalled look Ronan gives him speaks volumes. "I'm never teleporting again."

I wisely keep my mouth shut. He can fly, sure, but I stuck my head outside the cave one day last week, and the conditions out there are brutal. The wind especially. Before he can fly, he has to go outside, shift, and get off the ground, and that's not going to be fun with chunks of ice and snow pelting him in gale-force winds.

Fabian, who wandered off to peek into crates, chooses that moment to say, "Have you seen the preservation spells on this stuff? They're spectacular!"

"I saw them when I was here last time," Steffen says, but Wil goes to join Fabian.

Color is starting to return to Ronan's face, and his sips from the water bottle are getting longer. "Okay," he says at last, standing. "I'm sorry for the delay."

I pat his arm. "Don't worry about it. We're not on a schedule this afternoon."

Garrett comes to join us, followed by a blank-faced Zac and laughing Asher, and we give the dragons a tour of the cave. Then I explain what I'm doing with the puzzle and what I've discovered so far. Wil asks a lot of questions about the mechanical side of it, while Fabian seems more interested in the age of the pieces and what they're made of.

"We haven't checked," Garrett says. "We didn't want to risk taking any scrapings and then find out it affected the puzzle."

"But everything seems to be metal?" He's fascinated by that. "I'll check the living archive and see if there are any notes on what kind of metals were commonly used here back then."

I don't know what the living archive is, but if he can find out anything about the puzzle and the cave, that's gotta be a good thing.

Ronan's been quiet—probably not feeling well still—and I try to cheer him up. "Isn't this exciting? Soon I'll have the door open and you can start work. There's probably heaps of stuff in there about your culture and history! The anticipation must be killing you."

To my surprise, Ronan's face goes from unenthused to downright miserable. "Yeah."

I look over at Garrett, suddenly worried that I've said the wrong thing. He's frowning a little but gives me a reassuring nod.

"Before we go back to the village and get Ronan and Fabian settled, do you have any questions for Cam?"

"I have a list," Fabian declares, patting his pockets. He frowns. "Somewhere. Can I ask them later?"

"Sure," I assure him. "I'll be around."

"What's the plan moving forward?" Wil asks. "How soon do you anticipate the door being opened?"

Everyone looks at me. "Two to four weeks," I say confidently. "It depends on whether the pattern will change again. My money's on yes, and that will slow me down a little."

"That makes sense. Fabian will spend the next few days talking to people in the village, and when he leaves, Ronan will continue. If that's okay?"

I look over at Garrett. This is his area.

"Absolutely," he says. "Either I or Zac will introduce them around and help to facilitate things."

Steffen's habitual frown deepens. "Is that necessary? Will they face hostility?"

"Not hostility," Garrett's quick to reply. "But most people here haven't had a lot of experience with other species, and it can take them time to warm up. Plus demons are taciturn at the best of times."

"We are not," Zac gripes. Whatever Garrett said to him before seems to have put him in a bad mood.

"Regardless," Garrett continues, ignoring him, "having a familiar face to smooth the way can only help. Once people are used to seeing you"—he smiles at Fabian and Ronan. Fabian smiles back. Ronan doesn't—"there won't be any need for a facilitator."

That seems to satisfy Steffen. Nobody else has any questions, so Asher suggests we go back to the village.

"Where's the exit?" Ronan asks, looking around.

"Over there." Zac points, and Micah grabs his hand the same way he did to Isaac earlier.

"It might not be the best idea," he begins, shooting a worried look at Asher, but Ronan's already halfway to the entrance.

Steffen starts after him.

Ronan pauses when he sees the snow piled up inside the cave. We had a storm blow through during the week, and that always leaves a mess. It doesn't stop him, though, and he steps outside—

And then scrambles right back in, swiping snow out of his face. "How long have we been here? The weather's changed."

"Probably not," Garrett says gently. "The wind up here is pretty vicious. It's blowing all the snow around, but I doubt it's actually snowing. We're supposedly going to have a few clear days."

"So that's just the wind doing that?" He looks indecisively back at the entrance. Steffen steps outside for a moment. When he returns, he's frosted with snow all over, probably looking like I did after falling earlier.

"You can't fly in this," he says flatly. "Even Wil would hesitate to fly in this if he didn't have to."

Micah and Asher exchange glances, and I wonder what that's about.

Ronan doesn't look happy, but he grudgingly nods. "Fine."

"Come with me and Asher this time," Garrett suggests soothingly. "We'll go directly to the house we have ready for you, and you can have a proper rest."

As Ronan agrees and Asher teleports them away, I can't help thinking it seems like he really doesn't want to be here.

So why is he? Surely there's a dragon who would be excited about this?

𝕸

The minute we arrive in the village, my phone beeps loudly in my pocket. I force myself to ignore it while we make sure Fabian and Ronan are settled in, and then make plans to collect the dragons for dinner at Damaris's later. Wil and Steffen are leaving after that, but they assure us that they don't need daylight to fly.

Micah and I head back to our house for a break, and I wait until he's busy with the coffee maker to sneak my phone out of my pocket.

There are three messages waiting for me. One is from an Unknown Contact, and I don't even bother to open it. I don't need that kind of negativity in my life while I'm dealing with such a huge dilemma.

The other two messages are from Alistair, and I take a deep breath as I open the first one.

> Gideon talked to Micah and we had an emergency mini-meeting. Duuuuude! Operation: True Love is being disbanded. That demon has it baaaaaad for you. Our expert panel agrees that all you need to do is tell him how you feel. Trust me, you won't be disappointed.

> If you could video the declarations of love, we'd appreciate it.

I ignore that last part. No way am I sending Alistair video of me telling Micah I love him. Do I love him? Probably. If I'm not there yet, I will be soon.

"Micah?" My voice cracks, and I clear my throat as he

turns around. The concern on his face warms me all the way through, and suddenly I feel foolish. Of course he returns my feelings. How could I ever have doubted him?

"Is something wrong?"

I shake my head. "No. It's... I'm... I don't want to go home."

He pauses, then says slowly, "Well, there's still a lot to be done in the cave. But if you're worried about going back to that neighborhood, we can help you move."

Aww. How sweet and annoying. "No, it's not that. I meant I don't want to leave here."

A glint of excitement lights his eyes. "Oh?"

"I want to stay here." I take a breath. I'm confident he feels the way I do, but that doesn't stop the nerves. "With you. I want to be with you."

It only takes him two steps to reach me and sweep me up in the tightest, most wonderful hug I've ever experienced in my life.

"I'm never letting you go now."

# CHAPTER TWENTY-THREE

## Micah

I snuggle Cam closer to me on the couch, and he turns his head to kiss my cheek. We're lying under a blanket, supposedly watching a movie, but I don't think either of us has any clue what's actually going on. We've been too busy making out.

He's staying. Because he wants to be with me.

I've never been this happy before.

It makes me want to kick myself that I could have been feeling this sooner if I'd just told him I want him to stay. If I'd told him how I feel. Gideon will never let me live this down.

I chuckle. Gideon giving relationship advice is still the weirdest fucking thing ever.

"What's funny?" Cam asks, turning in my arms and nearly headbutting me in the cheekbone. My precious, clumsy man.

"I talked to Gideon this morning about you, and he said I should tell you how I feel. And I was just thinking that he's the last person anyone would usually go to for relationship support, but his advice turned out to be good."

To my surprise, his face goes fiery red.

"What?" I ask. "Should I not have talked to Gideon? I didn't say anything private."

He shakes his head. "No, that's fine. I..." He sits up suddenly, and only quick reflexes on my part keep him from being dumped on the floor. "I have a confession."

I sit up too, facing him. His face is serious, so this is important to him. But I can't think of anything he might say that would warrant a confession.

"I wasn't sure how to convince you that we belong together, so I called Alistair for advice. He put a mission team together and made Gideon call you to get inside intel."

What?

It takes me a lot longer than it should to process that. He called Alistair? And Alistair... made... Gideon...

I laugh.

Hard. And loudly.

"You're not mad?" Cam's relief breaks through my amusement, and I sweep him into my lap.

"Not mad," I promise, still chortling a little.

"Even though I spied on you?"

"Honestly, that just makes it all even better." I snort. "You cared enough to take action. And my cousin had to do something I bet he hated." This gives so much context to the call. No wonder he was such an ass.

"He really didn't want to do it," Cam tells me. "I would have felt bad for him if I didn't need the information so much."

"Neither of us is that bright, are we?" I ask, kissing his ear. "If we'd just communicated better, you wouldn't have had to ask Alistair for help. Though I'm glad you did. I can't wait to tell Asher and Zac that Gideon's been interfering in my love life."

He sighs. "I wish I had family like that. Someone I could torment but they still knew I loved them."

My arms tighten around him involuntarily, and he makes a small, wordless sound. "Sorry. I didn't mean to squeeze."

"I like it. I was just surprised. Squeeze away."

I do it again, but a little more gently this time. "You can torment my family," I offer. "In fact, you already did torment Gideon."

He chuckles, but it's wistful. "Yeah."

I don't say anything else—it would be an empty platitude right now, this early in our relationship. But I know it won't be long until he's so enmeshed in our family that the love-torment cycle comes naturally, and I can't wait to be able to give him that.

"You can ask me, you know," he says suddenly. "I don't mind talking about it."

"Your family?"

He nods.

"What happened?"

"They don't like me." He shrugs. "I didn't fit the mold they wanted me to, so I left home young—when I was around eighteen."

That *is* young for species as long-lived as ours. Plus, species like his—and vampires—tend to be even more protective of their young ones, since historically, feeding could be so dangerous. The modern era has made that easier for them, but old habits die hard.

"I'm sorry you didn't have their support." I imagine Isaac leaving at eighteen, *leaving* leaving, not just going away for schooling or adventure and still being in contact, and the thought makes me cold.

"It was better that way. They wanted me to join their social circle and be the life of the party and marry well and be... not me. I wanted to do my puzzles and have quiet fun with close friends. I was a puzzle piece that didn't fit, and leaving amicably was the best thing for all of us."

Dread swamps me. "There's more." It's not a question.

"Yeah." He slides his arms around my waist and leans his head against my shoulder. "About forty years ago, they reached out. They wanted us to have a closer bond, they said. My parents. They missed me, and could they visit? Take me out for a meal and catch up."

"You said yes." It sounds innocuous enough.

"Of course. I was... excited. When you have trouble making and keeping friends, it can get lonely sometimes. Even if we weren't ever going to be close, I liked the idea of having them in my life."

I give him another little squeeze.

"It was fine. They came to town, and we went to dinner. Things were a little awkward, but we left on a good note. They asked if I'd like to come visit for a weekend, and I agreed. My older sister had—has—children, and I wanted to meet them." He stops. Takes a breath. Shakes his head. "When I got there, they were having a house party. There were a dozen people or more staying in the house and the guest house. It wasn't what I'd expected, and even if I'd been prepared, it would have been overwhelming. Because, you see, many of the guests were the best and brightest business minds my father knew. Exactly the kind of person he wanted to leave his company to. And what better way to ensure that could happen than to keep it all in the family?"

My jaw drops. "They were planning to marry you off? For a business deal? When you hadn't been in contact with them for forty years?"

His head moves against me in a nod. "I didn't even realize until halfway through the second day when one of the eager contenders tried to convince me I should pick him. He was... handsy."

It's hard to keep my rage contained, but Cam doesn't need

me shouting right now. So I swallow it down. "He assaulted you?"

"I didn't think of it that way at the time, but yes. I got away from him before he could do more than grope me. When I went to grab my things and leave, I found that my parents had taken my car keys. They'd known I wouldn't want to stay, so they made sure I couldn't leave."

I bite my lip so hard, I taste blood, but give Cam another gentle squeeze. "What did you do?"

He lets out a little sigh and tips his head back to smile at me. "Thank you."

"What for?"

"For asking what *I* did. Not what they did. Not what happened next. What I did."

That hurts me more than anything else he's said. "You're an intelligent, capable man who can run his own life. I just want to be part of that. Maybe help out sometimes, share the load."

His smile widens. "I want that too." He leans his head back on my shoulder. "Part of being an intelligent, capable man is knowing when to ask for help. These were the days before cell phones, and I didn't even know the number for the local cab company. I could have called Enforcement, but my parents were—are—a big deal locally, and I wasn't sure that would work out for me. The only number I could remember off the top of my head right then was Alistair's. I figured he could at least help me arrange for a cab."

I remember what he said at lunch and suspect I'm about to find out why he has such high regard for Garrett's annoying cousin. "He helped you?"

"When I told him what was happening and asked if he could find me the number for a cab company, or a locksmith, he got all quiet—which should have been warning enough— then asked me for the address and told me he'd handle everything. 'Get your bags packed,' he said. 'You won't be there much longer.' And an hour later, he arrived with a bunch of other agents, mostly hellhounds and demons. He demanded my parents' hand over my keys, told them they were the stupidest people alive for not appreciating me, and then escorted me home." He sniffles, for the first time losing his composure. "And then he stayed with me for two days while I cried and wondered what was wrong with me."

It's a shame Alistair is such a pain in the ass, because he's now my brother and will always be welcome in my home. Oh well. I'm used to having relatives that piss me off. What's one more?

"There's nothing wrong with you," I say fiercely, even though I'm confident that he's past that point in his life.

He pats my chest. "I know. I'm comfortable with who I am now. And Alistair told me that a million times those first few days." He looks up at me. "I know he can be hard to take, but he really is a great friend. And his boyfriend keeps him pretty busy these days, so it's not likely he'll come to stay for a week or anything."

"If he does, he'll be welcome." I'm proud of myself for saying that without cringing. Cam must know what I'm thinking, because he laughs.

"Don't worry. We live in the same village as his cousin. He's much more likely to stay with Asher and Garrett than us."

I grin. Gideon giving love advice and Asher having to play host to Alistair? Cam's brought nothing but good things to my life.

"Alistair's right," I tell him. "Your family is stupid for not appreciating you. That's their loss. But I appreciate you, and my family loves you. You heard Isaac today. My mother would never get over it if I let you go. Even Grandmother likes you, and believe me, that's an achievement."

"She's not that bad." He hesitates. "Though dinner tonight was... interesting."

I scoff. "That's one word for it. I think Wil is the only dragon she kind-of liked. Definitely she was grateful that Asher talked her out of having Fabian and Ronan stay with her."

"I wonder what's going on with Ronan," Cam muses. "He obviously doesn't want to be here. At first I thought it was the location and the weather, but he doesn't even seem excited about the cave."

I noticed that too. The man's face looks like he's being punished in the worst way possible. "Maybe there's someone at home he doesn't want to be apart from," I suggest.

"Maybe. That still wouldn't explain why he's not even the tiniest bit interested in what's behind the puzzle. Fabian was super excited."

"I'm sure he'll settle in. He might be one of those people who doesn't show much on the outside. Steffen always looks like he thinks someone's about to attack him. Ronan's his brother—maybe his default is that he's miserable and uninterested."

That seems to cheer Cam up. "Like you demons with your faces!"

"There's nothing wrong with my face," I protest.

He grins, proclaims, "I like your face," and proceeds to kiss me all over it.

# CHAPTER TWENTY-FOUR

## Cam

"I'm kinda starting to get worried about him," I say to Zac, my gaze on Ronan as he talks to Arne at the bar. Fabian left on Wednesday, and Ronan's spent the time since talking to everyone who was involved in the decision to move the settlement here fifty years ago. The dragons are trying to find any information about the area that might point to what's in the cave. And if there isn't any, it's still good to have. Next week, he's going to fly to some longer-established towns and see what folklore he can pick up. We know that the area, and the village, are loosely named for the "hoard" that's here, so there's a good chance of dragon legends and lore too.

The only problem is that Ronan isn't trying to hide how miserable he is. People have noticed. At first they were sympathetic and extra nice to him, but that just seemed to make it worse.

"He's an adult," Zac says heartlessly. "He's not sick, just moody. He'll be fine."

Uh-huh. I'm not sure why people think he's the kind, gentle cousin. "Only two hours to go until Micah gets back," I mutter. He had a client meeting he couldn't put off any longer. He did manage to schedule it for Saturday so I wouldn't have to go to the cave with anyone else, which I appreciate—it would feel weird working with Zac or someone there. They don't know my system.

Micah also voluntold Zac to have lunch with me at the pub so I wouldn't get lonely or forget to eat. He's always thinking of little details like that.

Zac's been in a shitty mood all week, ever since Garrett told him off for being unsympathetic to Ronan. I think there's probably something else going on with him too, but I'm not sure if we're good enough friends for me to ask.

Of course, if we're not, he'll just snap at me. And since he's been alternating between snappy and apologetic for the last hour, that won't be anything new.

"What's going on with you?" I demand.

He has the gall to look surprised. "What do you mean?"

I roll my eyes. "You've been Grouchy McGrouchFace for days now. C'mon. We nearly dated. You can tell me."

To my relief, he laughs. "Next time Micah pisses me off, I'm going to remind him that Grandmother thought I was a better choice for you." He winks at me. "It's not too late, you know."

Knowing Zac as I do, I'm a hundred percent sure he's not propositioning me. "Not too late for what?"

"To tell Micah we've secretly fallen madly in love and want to be together."

A choking sound gets my attention, and I look up at Ronan. He's standing beside the table with wide eyes.

"Hey, Ronan! Join us. Have you had lunch?"

He takes a step back, gaze swinging from me to Zac and back again. "No, thanks. I just wanted to s-say... uh. To ask if I can come to the cave one day next week?"

"Of course. Just let us know which day and we'll bring you

with us." I smile brightly at him, hoping to make him feel more at ease.

He nods and takes another step back. "Okay. Thank you."

"Won't you sit with us and have a drink?" I ask again. I don't think I've seen him be social at all this week, and that can't be a good thing.

Ronan shakes his head. "No, I have stuff to do. I'll talk to you later." He turns and practically flees.

"I'm so worried about him," I tell Zac as I stare after him.

"Meh. You know he thinks we're having a secret affair."

I blink and give him my full attention. "What? Why?"

"Because that's what we were talking about when he walked up."

"But..." I glance toward the door Ronan went through. "But that was a joke."

Zac shrugs. "He didn't get it."

Oh well. "I'll sort it out later. Or he'll realize it was a joke."

"I don't know. He doesn't strike me as a person who has a sense of humor."

Which brings me back to my original point. "Yeah, he's not happy, and I'm worried about him. But I'm also worried about you. What's going on with you?"

"Since when do you notice anything that's not a puzzle or Micah?" he demands.

"Stop deflecting." I will not be distracted.

"I'm not. There's nothing going on with me."

I give him a stern look. Or I try to. It doesn't seem to have any effect. He might even be smiling.

Before I can order him to talk to me, someone slides into one of the other chairs at our table. My hope that Ronan changed his mind is dashed when I glance over and see Arne.

"Hi." I sound surprised because I am surprised. "I don't think I've ever seen you out from behind the bar." Now that I think of it, does he have a lower half? I mean, he must, but I wish I'd caught a glimpse before he sat down.

"I do spend most of my life there," he jokes. At least, I think it's a joke. In typical demon manner, his face stays mostly blank. It's hard to read tone without visual cues. "Listen, I need to talk to you. Or Garrett, but he hasn't come in today and I don't have time to find him."

Uh-oh. "What's wrong?" If he needs to talk to me or Garrett, either there's a problem with the cave, or he's planning to leave the village and live in the outside world. Considering how much people love the pub, neither is a good option.

"That Ronan guy."

"Ronan?" Okay, that's not what I was expecting. "What's wrong with him? Did he say something rude?"

Arne hesitates. "It's not what he says. He doesn't say anything much, just asks his questions and writes things down."

I nod encouragingly and wish Zac would step in. This is why things would never have worked out between us. Micah would have done something supportive by now—put a hand on my leg or shoulder or at least moved his chair closer, so I knew he was there if I needed him. I'm not even sure if Zac's listening. What if I blunder and say something that destroys incubus-demon relations for centuries? Would he at least step in then?

"He's documenting things that might help us when we publicize the cave," I say, even though he knows that. It's been explained several times.

"I don't know that we want any documentation he has a hand in. What's he going to say about us?"

Wow. Okay. This is way above my skill level. I shoot Zac a panicked look.

"I don't understand," he says to Arne, who makes a face that even I can see.

"A few of us have gotten a strong impression that he doesn't like us. Demons, not us specifically. That Fabian was a good sort, but Ronan doesn't want to be here, doesn't want to talk to us, doesn't even want to breathe the same air as us."

"You think he's speciesist?" Zac asks carefully while I try not to panic. This is not good. Not good at all. We need a dragon here to go through the contents of the cave. It's an important part of the plan to integrate Hortplatz with the rest of the community. I might not even officially live here yet, but it's my home, dammit, and I won't let this plan be derailed!

"He can't be," I blurt. "He's just antisocial. He doesn't spend much time talking to me or Garrett either." Too late, I realize that wasn't the flex I was hoping for.

"Because he's antisocial, or because you're not dragons?" Arne asks. I scramble with my mouth open to think of something to say, but there's nothing. He pats my hand. "You're a good sort, Cam, and you always want to think the best of everyone. But not everyone is as good as you."

Fuck. *Fuck*. If people complain to the council about Ronan, there's every chance they'll ask to have him replaced. Rejecting non-demons from the village because of personality clashes isn't a great way to tell the world we want them to come here.

Unless... could Ronan be speciesist? I think back over every interaction I've had with him, and I really don't think that's it. I've touched him casually a few times in conversation, and he's never shied away. He looks unhappy to be here, but not disdainful or antagonistic.

"How many of you feel this way?" Zac asks, and Arne shrugs.

"Pretty much everyone he's spoken to more than once,"

he says. "They elected me to say something about it. We don't want to make it official and cause trouble, but if you could have a word with him, maybe he could ask to be transferred? It would make everyone happy."

"I'll definitely have a word," Zac promises, and something in his tone makes me pull my phone out of my pocket and text Garrett under the table.

r u home? Problem

"We don't need to be dealing with this kind of attitude in our own home," Arne is saying. "We don't want to cause trouble, but we will if we have to."

My phone rings in my hand, and I answer it with relief. "Garrett! Hi."

"What's wrong?" he asks frantically. "Are you hurt?"

"I'm fine," I assure him, smiling big at Zac and Arne. "But actually, Zac and I might come over. We have something to talk to you about."

"Zac? Why... oh that's right, Micah's in Milan. Okay, come over. Can you give me a hint? Do we want coffee or something stronger?"

"Something stronger, for sure." I end the call on his moan. "Thanks for bringing this to our attention, Arne. We'll discuss it with Garrett and make a plan."

He doesn't look convinced, so I follow up with my brightest smile and push back my chair to stand. Unfortunately, I somehow get my foot tangled in it and nearly fall.

"Are you okay?" Zac asks as my chair goes flying and I catch myself on the table with my forearm. Ouch.

"All good," I declare, looking around for my chair and gratefully seeing that it caused no damage. "We better go. Garrett's waiting."

Hopefully, he'll have an idea to fix this.

# CHAPTER TWENTY-FIVE

## Micah

Asher wasn't clear in his text about why I needed to get home as soon as possible, but I still didn't waste any time. Luckily, my meeting was wrapping up anyway. I got the client's signoff on the new drawings, shook hands, promised an update soon, and got out of there.

Now, as I step out of the teleport room at the house I share with my cousins, I wonder what could possibly have happened in just a few hours. At least Cam's okay—Zac would have been the one to message me if something had happened to him.

Raised voices lead me to the kitchen, where Cam and Zac are facing down while Garrett and Asher watch. I may have spoken too soon.

Is... is Garrett recording this? I can't think why else he'd have his phone pointed at them.

"Hello?" I call, pitching it to cut through Cam's shout that Zac's a stupid, intolerant shit-for-brains. All heads turn toward me. "What's going on?"

Cam, Zac, and Garrett all start speaking at once, the

words jumbling together in a wall of nonsensical sound. Asher just sneers.

I dump my folio on the kitchen table and fold my arms across my chest. "One at a time. No yelling. Cam?"

Zac scoffs, and I shoot him a glare. What the fuck is wrong with everyone?

Sniffing in disdain, Cam says, "Everybody in the village thinks Ronan is speciesist and wants him out. But he's just unhappy, Micah, I know it. We can't let him think he's not wanted." He sounds on the verge of tears, and I have to wonder if maybe this has hit a sore spot for him. He doesn't know Ronan well enough to be so emotional otherwise.

Before I can ask for details, Zac interrupts. "You don't know that he's unhappy." He sounds exasperated, like he's said this a few times already. "All we know is that he's being an ass."

Cam immediately starts yelling again. I meet Asher's gaze, and he raises a brow as if to say "See?"

I put my arm around Cam and tug him against my side. He immediately looks up at me. "He's not speciesist."

"Why don't you tell me exactly what happened?" I suggest, wondering how this became my mess. "Zac, not a word until he's done, or I swear, I'll tell Garrett's cousin Alistair you want to go to karaoke with him."

Garrett perks up. "Karaoke?"

"Not right now," Asher tells him.

Cam explains exactly what happened while I was gone, then adds on all the reasons why he thinks Ronan is just a miserable person, and not a bigoted one. I can't help frowning. This is an all-around shitty situation. There's no way to resolve it without talking to Ronan and potentially offending him. Scratch that—definitely offending him. I don't care so much about that if it turns out he *is* a bigot, but I'm inclined to agree with Cam on this. Which means we're about to tell a man that the village thinks he's a bigot and wants him gone.

"Garrett, this is really your department, as the project coordinator and liaison." I look at him hopefully.

"I hate you," he says. "But fine. I'll talk to Ronan. The thing is... what outcome do we want here? If he's speciesist, I can make a case to everyone else that he's not the best person to be working on this project. But if he's not... I can't tell them the village decided he's not welcome here because he's not a happy person."

We all wince at the same time. It would be funny if the situation wasn't so fucked-up.

"Let's talk to him first," Zac suggests. "He's a miserable bastard and I bet there's a decent chance that's because he thinks he's better than us, but let's find out for sure before we do anything drastic. Maybe he's just having a bad week and can make an effort to improve his mood."

Cam huffs. "That's what I've been saying! Micah never has to worry about me running away with you, because I could never handle the mood swings!" He tosses his head, setting his curls to dancing.

"Um... what?" He and Zac have talked about running away together?

"Never mind," Zac tells me with a roll of his eyes.

"I don't know why I married into this family, but since I did, we're having karaoke night tonight. You all have to participate." Garrett points at each of us in turn to emphasize his point, and dread curdles in my stomach.

"Karaoke? Really?" I protest weakly. "I didn't do anything. I wasn't even here."

Cam gives me big eyes. "You don't want to do karaoke with us?"

"I..."

His eyes widen even more, and he pouts.

"Fine. Karaoke." I glare at Asher. If he hadn't married Garrett, I wouldn't be in this position. "There had better be alcohol."

"Believe me, there will," he says fervently.

Garrett claps his hands. "Great! Asher and I are going to talk to Ronan. Zac, you're cooking dinner."

"Why me?"

"Because you were half of the pain in my ass today, and the other half doesn't know how to cook."

There's a pause. "Does that make me the other half of the pain in your ass?" Cam asks. "That's so unfair. I was just trying to prevent an interspecies incident. Imagine how bad it would be if the village kicked out the representative of the dragon wing leader for no reason."

That wouldn't be good. Especially when this is a three-way project with CSG. The last thing we need is angry government representatives demanding to know why we're fucking things up.

Although, that angry rep would probably be Gideon.

Which reminds me... "Nobody's said anything about this to the council or Grandmother yet, have they?"

"Arne was pretty clear that they didn't want to make it official yet," Zac confirms. "We have time to sort it out."

I nod. "Good. Hopefully, she never has to know."

ЭDℓ

Maybe it makes me a bad person, but I was really hoping Garrett and Asher would come back with bad news. Either that Ronan is, in fact, a bigot, or that he's so offended by the suggestion that he's leaving in a huff and we created an interspecies incident with the dragons. Because as horrible as both those things would be, they would also get me out of karaoke night.

What would be worse, insulting the dragons and causing political mayhem, or karaoke with a hellhound? It's hard to say.

But they returned with, if not smiles, at least relief. Garrett wouldn't share the details, and Asher won't risk upsetting Garrett, but they did say that Ronan isn't speciesist and has promised to make more of an effort. That's the best we can ask for, really. Even if it does mean we're currently setting up for a karaoke tournament.

A fucking tournament. Because it's not enough that we need to sing for no good reason, we also have to compete against each other.

It's hard to stay mad, though, when I see how excited Cam is. He and Garrett have cast from Garrett's karaoke app (which apparently no hellhound goes without) to the big TV in the living room, and they're scrolling through the song selection. Garrett's leaning more toward Billie Holiday and Celine Dion, while Cam's declared he's going through an Adele phase.

Zac brings me a bottle of shifter brew, and I take it eagerly. I don't normally drink that much, but I feel like alcohol is going to be needed to get me through tonight. "Thank you."

"I'd say you're welcome, but what I really want to know is why I'm here," my cousin grumbles. "I don't have a karaoke-loving boyfriend to make happy."

"True," I agree. "But if you leave and it makes *my* karaoke-loving boyfriend unhappy, I'll make sure you regret it forever." Pleasure thrills through me when I refer to Cam as my boyfriend. *My* boyfriend. It's been a week since we agreed that's what we are to each other, and the joy of it still hasn't worn off. "Speaking of my boyfriend, we're going to need your help moving his stuff. I'll let you know when." We haven't worked out the details yet, but Cam wants to stay focused on getting the puzzle solved first. That should still give us time to work out the logistics of him moving here and get it done before he needs to start work again.

Zac huffs. "Oh, yay. I finally get to realize my lifelong dream of being a pack mule." He shoots me a sidelong smile. "Seriously, you and Asher are so lucky I don't hate you."

"Don't hate us because you're jealous," I say mock-solemnly, my gaze on Cam's happy face. "Grandmother's already thinking about who she can match you with. And your mom is helping her."

He rolls his eyes. "Don't remind me. Maybe I should have convinced Cam to fake date me that night at dinner. Then they'd be switching their focus to you, and I could go on my merry way."

I shake my head. "No, that wouldn't have worked."

"Why not?"

"Because I'd have killed you." I smile widely, and he laughs.

"You'd have tried." He pauses. "But maybe I should give more thought to fake dating someone. It worked for Asher."

We both look over at Asher, who's listening to Garrett explain that he needs to pick his "signature karaoke style" with a besotted expression on his face.

"Only with more emphasis on the fake part," Zac adds. "Too bad there's nobody."

I consider that. He's right in the sense that anyone local who knows Grandmother would probably either flat-out refuse to deceive her or break down when faced with her and confess all. That would be bad. But... "What about Ronan?" I suggest, tongue-in-cheek. "He's new and will be here for at least a few months. You could tell Grandmother there's a connection between you and delay any serious attempts at her setting you up with someone else."

Zac's shaking his head before I'm even done talking. "That's a firm no."

"Oh?" He's not usually this easy to torment. "But why? I think he'd be an excellent fake match for you." I hide my smile as he glances scornfully at me.

"He wouldn't. I can't stand being in the same room as him. There's no way I could convince anyone I was attracted to him. Not that he'd agree anyway. He's a miserable son of a bitch with no sense of humor."

I'm taken aback by both his words and his tone. I knew Zac didn't like Ronan—I'm not exactly a fan of him myself—but this seems to go beyond that.

Before I can think of a way to ask why he hates him so much, he continues, "Maybe I should invent a fake boyfriend like you did for Asher. Only I'll be careful not to use any names or details of real people."

"Where would you have met them?" I ask reasonably. "It worked—kind of—for Asher because he spends so much time in Zurich. You spend all your time here or somewhere else on the mountain. Unless your secret fake boyfriend is a hermit living in a cave, nobody's going to believe you have a relation-ship you just haven't mentioned."

"Whose boyfriend is a hermit in a cave?" Cam asks, bounding over to us and nearly tripping on the corner of the coffee table. I catch his arm and steady him.

"Nobody's. We're just joking about Zac's lack of a dating life."

Cam makes a sympathetic face. "I bet you're feeling lonely now that your two closest cousins are hooked up," he commiserates. "Don't worry, Zac. Garrett and I would never make them cut you out, would we, Garrett?"

"No way," Garrett declares emphatically. "We're all family now. Hey, we should make karaoke night a regular family event!"

Zac's eyes widen, but before he can say anything, Cam adds, "Pub trivia too. That's so much fun. And maybe once the snow starts to clear and more people are coming to see the village, we can find someone special for Zac. Garrett, do you know anyone we could set him up with?"

They start talking about people they know who would be "perfect for an outdoorsy demon," and Zac slowly turns a horror-filled look my way.

"You made it *worse*."

# CHAPTER TWENTY-SIX

## Cam

It's been thirteen days since the topic came up at karaoke night, but for some reason, any time I try to talk to Micah or Zac about getting him back into the dating market, they shut me down. It's almost like Zac doesn't want to meet someone amazing and be stupid happy.

Weird.

I push the thought aside. There'll be plenty of time for me to help Zac after I move here and the village becomes a popular destination for visitors of all species... which is going to happen soon, because today's the day I finish the puzzle.

Today. *Today*.

I knew last week how much longer it would take me, but I deliberately didn't tell anyone because I didn't want to start a tidal wave of excitement. Instead, I kept it to myself—and Micah, because I tell him everything now—and kept working. Even when Ronan spent three days with us in the cave last week, cataloging all the components and watching me work, I didn't tell him. I'm pretty sure he guessed how close I was, though, given he could see my progress each day.

But when we left the cave last night, I knew it would be

today and that a lot of people would want to be here. So I told Garrett.

He freaked out. "Tomorrow?" he kept saying. "Like in twelve hours, tomorrow?"

"Probably closer to nineteen or twenty," I corrected. "I don't think I'll be done until early afternoon."

He took that and ran with it, understanding without me needing to tell him that I didn't want a dozen or more people watching my every move the whole morning.

Instead, they'll start arriving after lunch. The village council and someone from CSG—Garrett thinks probably Alistair and Gideon. More people will come later, when the door is open and Ronan's going through what's behind it, but Garrett's promised to keep things low-key today.

Which means I can work mostly in peace this morning. It's not as peaceful as usual, though—Micah, Asher, Garrett, Zac, and Ronan are stacking the now-empty crates along the side wall of the cave. That's where they were in the photos I saw right after the cave was discovered. It makes the cave seem a lot bigger—not that it didn't already feel huge—and will allow us to actually open the door.

I stop to watch them work. Zac, who was the sunshiny one when I first met them all but has lost his good humor these last few weeks, is keeping up a steady stream of muttered curses. He's also avoiding Ronan like it's his job, which makes me sad. Ronan's been trying really hard since Garrett talked to him. He even made a point of visiting the people he'd interviewed and apologizing for his mood. He told them he'd been dealing with some stuff in his life that had left him unprepared to move out here on such short notice, but he hadn't meant to take that out on everyone else, and that he thought the village was one of the friendliest and most inviting places to live that he'd seen in a long time. Personally, I think that last bit was overkill, seeing as how the people he said it to were trying to get him kicked out of the village, but they bought it, and combined with his new efforts to be more social, it's made a difference.

Micah glances over at me and winks, and I grin and wave at him. We're both super excited right now. Once the door is open, we can start planning what comes next for us. I'll move to Hortplatz, and we can slowly take our relationship to the next level. It's given us both a boost of enthusiasm for today, and seeing how excited we already were, that makes us positively giddy. I take a few more seconds to watch his muscles flex as he and Asher maneuver another crate over to the winch. They're much lighter empty, but still awkward and unwieldy.

I get back to work, focusing on fitting components into elements. The puzzle still occasionally likes to throw me a curveball and mix things up, but for the most part, I know what pieces go where and how they need to be moved. Now, especially, with so few pieces left, there aren't a lot of potential combinations with each step. I'm working in the bottom right corner, so the cherry picker that was my best friend for the past few weeks has been moved to the staging area of the cave, out of my way, leaving an unimpeded view of my work.

It's impressive.

That's not me bragging. I know that I'm just bringing someone else's genius to life—and she really was a genius. But if the door was a marvel of engineering before, it's a downright work of art now. The relief image of the dragon, wings spread, is spectacular, right down to the cheeky smirk on its face. I wonder if it's a self-portrait? I asked Ronan, but he said he'd never met the designer and didn't know.

I pick up the pace a little. I'm so close to the end now, following one last spiral of the tail. In fact... I stop, make myself put down the component I was about to place, and take a step back.

"Something wrong?" Micah steps up beside me, lightly sweaty, and I turn into him, plastering myself against his big body.

"Nope. But there's only about half an hour of work left, and I thought I should probably wait for everyone to get here."

He looks up at the wall, at the progress. "I can't believe it's nearly over."

"Nearly done," I correct. "Not over. Once it's open, I want to experiment to see if pieces can be removed without closing it."

His familiar chuckle washes over me. "I can see you're going to be playing with this for a long time."

A long time here with Micah? You fucking bet.

ꟅꟅ

I can feel all the eyes on me as I solve the last of the puzzle. At first they watched me in deathly silence, but the weight of that was so bad that I asked them to please talk. So there's a quiet murmur of conversation, at least.

Those who haven't visited since I started working—which is most people—were shocked and delighted to see how the door looks now. The dragon wing leader, Brandt, who surprised us all by tagging along with Gideon, actually clapped his hands in joy. "This is extraordinary!" he exclaimed. "I should have known she'd find a way to turn one art form into two."

He's been talking to Ronan, and I hope they're working on a way to resolve whatever it is that's making Ronan so unhappy.

But that's not what I'm supposed to be focused on. I slot what ostensibly should be the last piece into the last element, twist it, and slide. It locks into place just like all the ones before.

"Is that it?" someone asks. "I thought it would be more dramatic. Can we open it now?"

I shake my head and don't bother to turn around as I hold up the two components that are "leftover." "I have to find a home for these first."

There's a moment of shocked silence. I'm pretty sure they're all wondering if I missed a piece somewhere, like putting together DIY furniture. They don't understand that it would be impossible to do that with this puzzle—the sequence has to be exact. If I didn't put the right piece in the right place, I wouldn't be able to move on to the next step. I don't waste time explaining, just bend to examine the spot where I placed the previous component. If my guess is right, these last two pieces will act as a handle for the door. I just don't know where the handle is supposed to be.

"Excuse me, Ronan," I call over my shoulder. "Could I borrow you for a moment?"

There's a flurry of whispers as Ronan comes to stand beside me. I try not to be annoyed by my observers. "How can I help?" he asks quietly.

"What's the standard design layout of a dragon door?" I ask, keeping my voice low. "And has it changed over time? Like, would the designer have laid it out differently all those millennia ago to how someone might do it now?"

He hesitates. "Uh—"

"Sorry," a cheerful voice interrupts as Wing Leader Brandt joins us. "So sorry, but I'm nosy and desperate to see what's inside. How can I help?"

I don't miss the stark relief that crosses Ronan's face, but with Brandt waiting, I don't have time to ask. I explain what I need to know.

He nods. "We dragons don't have a special door design. We just steal things like that from the elves, since they'd already done the hard work before we even decided to change forms."

Does that even make sense? He's still talking, though.

"The doors we had were basically the same as what you have on Earth. A rectangle with a handle."

"It's the handle placement I need to know," I tell him. "Left or right side of the door? Or in the middle?"

He cocks his head. "Huh. I... Hold on." While everyone watches, he closes his eyes and extends a hand as though reaching for a door handle. "Left side," he declares. "Definitely the left side."

"Thank you." That means I'm on the wrong side, so I turn around and walk along the face of the door to the other side. "Have all the photos been taken?" I call. This might take me a while to figure out, or I might be done in thirty seconds. Better to get the process moving.

"All photos are done," Micah says, coming over to me. "Anything you need?"

I smile at him. I didn't think of it, but I'm glad he'll be with me for the last pieces. I hold them up. "We're looking for a notch or somewhere these will fit. I talked to Ronan when he was here last week, and he agrees that it wouldn't be possible to solve the puzzle in dragon form, so it's likely to be somewhere within arm's reach of a standard biped."

We start looking. After so many hours working on it, the vagaries of the door are as familiar to me as the lines of my hands. This shouldn't take too long—I'm actually surprised I didn't notice the abnormality while I was working in this area.

"Cam?" Micah murmurs. "Could this be it?"

I turn so fast, I overbalance and fall sideways into the wall. Micah grabs me before I fully hit it, saving me from a massive headache. I can handle a small bruise to my upper arm, but my skull wouldn't have enjoyed all those metal components.

"Thanks!" I lean up and kiss him, to a chorus of gasps. Oops. Oh well... screw professional propriety. "Show me."

The irregular spot he points out could be a production error. The door was made by hand, and sometimes tools slip. But... I press my pinky finger to it and realize it's deeper than it looks, and angled.

I look again at the two components in my hand. If I fit them together like so, and then... I slide the end of the "handle" into the depression. It doesn't work, so I pull back and change the angle slightly.

This time, it slides in properly and clicks into place. My heart starts to beat harder. This is really it.

"Who—" I stop to clear my throat. "Who wants the honors?"

"You'll do it," Damaris says immediately, her tone brooking no argument. I glance over my shoulder to see her aiming a gimlet stare at everyone else. "You've earned it."

Nobody disagrees.

I turn back to the handle and glance up at Micah.

"Are you ready?" he asks, and I know he's asking about more than just the door.

There's no doubt in my mind when I say, "Yes," and pull down the handle.

# CHAPTER TWENTY-SEVEN

## Micah

I don't think I'm the only one holding my breath as Cam pulls the handle down. There's a very audible click.

And then nothing.

"Is it rusted closed?" Jesse asks behind me. "The hinges probably aren't in good shape."

"The preservation spell should have maintained them in the same state as the rest of the door," Brandt says, but there's a note of worry in his voice.

"It's fine," Cam assures them calmly. "I haven't pulled yet."

The sigh of relief that goes through the group is quite gusty. Cam adjusts his grip on the handle, and I see his knuckles tighten as he pulls. The door moves fractionally... I think. It's hard to tell.

Bracing himself, Cam glances at me. "Lend me some muscle?"

I put both hands over his and brace as well. "On three?"

"One. Two. Three."

We pull.

The door slowly, ponderously swings toward us. It's heavy, and I think the hinges might need some love too—which, after so long, is to be expected—but it's moving. Cam and I scramble back out of the way.

The door turns out to be six inches thick. I don't know *that* much about history, but I'm pretty sure nobody on Earth was forging metal when the dragons were last here. It was definitely created by dragon magic.

As it swings past us, I look over to the cave wall opposite. "Should we try to catch it?" If it hits the wall, the puzzle might be damaged.

Even as Asher and Gideon spring forward, the door's momentum slows. It comes to a stop just as it kisses the wall.

We turn our attention to what was behind it.

"Wow," someone breathes, and I want to echo it.

The cave extends for perhaps another fifty feet. It's twenty feet wide and twenty feet high, and the walls are lined with neatly constructed wood shelves stacked to the brim with... things. Down the middle, there's a wide ten-foot-long table, and beyond that, more shelves, dividing the room into two sections. Everything looks to be in good condition.

"We should go in," Grandmother says, but for once she doesn't sound certain.

"Brandt?" Garrett suggests. "Would you do the honors?"

I take Cam's hand and we stand at the threshold as Brandt steps forward and crosses into the... cave. Hm. The cave-within-the-cave? This could get confusing. He walks into the hoard, breathes deeply, and then goes to the table.

"There's a message," he says, his voice cracking a little.

"What does it say?" Garrett's holding up his phone, recording everything, and tears are streaming down his cheeks. He's such a good teacher that I forget sometimes he's also a social anthropologist, and this must be a dream come true for him.

"Hoarded here be the treasures of all, kept for some whim

yet unknown." He looks over at us and shrugs. "It's not signed, but I recognize the magical residue."

We crowd forward to see for ourselves. The message is burned into the tabletop, symbols I don't recognize. I know that while humans believe the earliest signs of written language date back around six thousand years, we in the community were using it before then, but not as far back as we suspect this cave was set up.

"Some whim yet unknown," Jesse muses. "I wonder if she could have been feeling the influence of the magic? There are times I do things I don't fully understand because I feel it guiding me."

"Highly possible," Brandt agrees. "Though we'll likely never know or understand why it wanted a collection of objects that would be lost for millennia."

"They're found now," Gideon says in hushed tones as he gazes around at the shelves. "Sam isn't going to believe this. He's so mad he couldn't be here."

"Can we..." I give Cam's hand a little squeeze as he pauses. "Could we look at something? I know we need to be careful and everything needs to be documented, but could we look at just one thing?"

Garrett lowers his phone. "I don't see why not."

After a short debate, we decide to keep things as orderly as possible and choose from one of the shelves at the front. First, we move some of the lights from the outer part of the cave, giving us better visibility. Then Garrett lifts down a wrapped object, about a foot long and six or so inches wide, and Ronan takes over recording as he carries it to the table and unwraps it.

Inside is a clay tablet with markings on it. It looks wrong, somehow, and then I realize that's because all the pictures I've ever seen of clay tablets show a lot of wear and tear. This looks like it could have been made yesterday. None of us can read the markings.

"It's from Earth, then," Brandt says. He sounds calm, but he's grinning widely. "I would recognize any dragon or elven markings from that time."

"I'll check it against known languages when we get back to Wi-Fi," Garrett says as he and Ronan carefully document everything and rewrap the clay slab. "Shall we take a walk around?" He gestures toward the back of the hoard.

Ronan returns the tablet to where we found it, and then, as a group, we stroll down one aisle. Beside me, Cam takes a deep breath.

"What?" I murmur, and he shakes his head.

"Being in the middle of it all really brings home how much there is. Look at all this stuff. It's going to change history as we know it."

He's right. And our village—us... we're going to be part of that.

It sends a shiver down my spine, but a good one.

When we've walked both aisles, Garrett and Ronan recording and taking preliminary notes, we return to the door and better lighting. I'm surprised to see that Jesse and Brandt are both a little teary-eyed.

"This is incredible," Jesse says. "And the magic is so... it's so happy we've found this again."

"Ecstatic," Brandt adds. "Euphoric. If there was cell service here, I'm sure we'd be getting calls from the lucifer and the elf king to ask us what we found, it's that thrilled."

"Hmm," Garrett murmurs. "We're going to need to see about getting cell service up here. The sooner, the better. Ronan's not going to be able to work effectively if he can't look things up easily or call people for information."

"He can fly," Zac points out flatly, but the glares that are aimed at him make him subside.

"The conditions outside the cave aren't good for that yet,"

Garrett reminds him with narrowed eyes. "And even if they were, having to fly somewhere with cell service every time he has to check something isn't efficient."

"We'll get cell service for the cave," Grandmother insists, cutting any discussion short. "Isn't that right, Jesse? We do whatever is needed to bring this treasure to the world." Her expression is fierce, daring anyone to challenge her.

"Of course," Jesse confirms quickly. "Garrett, Ronan, just let us know what you need." He looks around. "The rest of us should probably go so you can make plans to get started."

It hits me with a pang that Cam and I are part of "the rest of us" now. Sure, Cam needs to mess around with the door a little now that it's open, see how it functions, but for the most part, our job here is done.

"If I could just interject," Brandt says slowly. "You mentioned that the conditions outside aren't ideal for flying, and I don't doubt that, given our location and the season. But how will Ronan be traveling back and forth from the cave, now that Micah and Cam are done here? Should I call in a favor with the king and have an elf assigned to portal him?"

Ronan's face relaxes in pure relief, the happiest I've ever seen him.

"That won't be necessary." Grandmother leaps in so quickly, it takes me a second to even realize she's spoken. "Until the weather improves, Zac will be working with Ronan and Garrett."

As if we're all puppets on a string, Cam, Asher, Garrett, Gideon, and I turn to look at Zac. His expression is a study in bewilderment. "I will?"

"He will?" Garrett echoes. Ronan says nothing, but his face closes.

"Is that a problem?" Grandmother asks Zac in a tone that warns him to think carefully about his answer. "Do you not want to join your cousins in doing your part for our village and the Community of Species?"

"Doing my part?" Zac echoes. "What did Asher do? I don't think he married Garrett for the good of the Community of Species, Grandmother."

"Asher knows his duty," Grandmother intones, and Asher shoots me an alarmed look, mouthing, "My duty?" I shrug.

Zac opens his mouth to argue, thinks better of it, and shrugs. "Sure. I can bring Garrett and Ronan back and forth and help out. But only until the weather changes. I can't be stuck in this cave during the summer."

Grandmother flips a hand dismissively. "When the snow starts to clear, we can make other arrangements. Perhaps some kind of vehicle to travel up from the village?"

"No." Zac's voice is firm. "A vehicle would cause environmental damage in the woods, and it's a slippery slope from one, to many, to cutting down trees to accommodate a road. Besides, even in the summer the conditions above the tree line aren't always good for vehicles. It would be too unreliable."

Cam leans against me, taking in the impromptu family drama. Grandmother doesn't look happy, but she nods curtly, conceding to Zac's greater knowledge about the area and the necessary safety concerns. "We'll make other arrangements. We have time to sort them out. It's not even spring yet, and I think this year the snow will linger into June."

Nobody says anything, but those of us who know her well are probably all thinking the same thing: What the heck is she basing that on?

Brandt claps his hands. "That's all arranged, then. Excellent. Gideon, I just need a word with Ronan, and then we can go back to CSG, if that suits you."

"Of course," Gideon says politely, and then as Brandt draws Ronan aside, he makes a beeline toward Zac.

"Are we going to go listen to them?" Cam murmurs. "Is Gideon telling him off or giving him advice?"

I tug him along with me and head in that direction. "Knowing Gideon, probably both." Sure enough, as we get closer, I hear Gideon call Zac an idiot and then follow up with, "I'm not going to mourn you if you get killed by a dragon." Other people might not consider that advice, but from Gideon, it really is. It's loving, even. I crash the conversation before anything else can be said.

"What's with you lately?" I ask Zac. "I can't believe you argued with Grandmother over this. You're only doing research and reading right now, and you can do that from here while Garrett and Ronan work."

His face sets in mutinous lines. "Maybe I don't want to sit in a cave when I can be in my comfortable house."

Gideon and I roll our eyes in perfect unison. "I did it," I point out.

"You were getting sex," he snaps. "Maybe if someone offered to fuck me, I'd be more on board with this." His voice rises slightly at the end, and over his shoulder, I see Garrett's head snap around. Nobody else seems to notice, though, thankfully.

"Keep it down," Gideon warns, obviously having noticed the same thing as me. "We don't want an inter-species incident."

I try not to wince, since he doesn't know about how narrowly we avoided the last one.

Zac sighs. "I just wish someone would care about my opinion."

"We do," Cam says earnestly. "I got distracted before, but you still need to tell me what's wrong."

"Something's wrong?" Gideon asks sharply.

"No," Zac replies, even as Cam says, "Yes."

"Nothing's wrong," Zac insists. "I guess winter's just

getting to me this year. I'd go spend a week on a beach, but now I've been voluntold for taxi and babysitting duty."

Cam immediately begins assuring him that he can take a couple of days off to go to the beach, since there are still some things he wants to do here in the cave, and I can be the taxi-slash-babysitter. But I tune most of that out. Zac might've been able to distract my boyfriend, but I know him too well, and that was absolutely a lie.

Gideon meets my gaze. He knows it too. Something's going on with Zac.

I stare at my list in frustration. It's too short—I know it is. There's a lot more stuff I'm gonna need to set up my work-room here in Hortplatz. But damned if I can remember what all that stuff is.

Oh well. When I get to the house and see it, I'll know what to grab. It's just annoying that my brain won't let me be organized as I take this huge step and move in with my sexy demon boyfriend.

"Ready?" Micah asks, coming out of the kitchen. I grin at him.

"Yep! I—"

His phone rings, and he frowns.

"Get it," I tell him. "We're not in a rush." We're really not. Today I'm just going through my stuff and deciding what needs to come back now. We'll bring what we can carry, but the rest we'll pack up ready for when Micah's cousins are going to help.

He still doesn't look happy as he takes the call, and from the sound of what he's saying as he wanders back into the kitchen, his mood's not going to improve. That's so sweet. He's mad that people are taking away from his time with me.

Oooh—time! I add clockwork pieces to my list. I don't often use them, but they can be fun, and I don't store them with everything else.

"...hold on," Micah says as he comes back into the room, then taps the screen—I'm guessing to mute the call. "My client's builder has fucked up and I need to go to the site. Is it okay if—"

"Take me home and leave me there," I assure him. "I can manage until you come back. Just don't forget me."

"Like I'd ever do that," he mutters, unmuting the call. "Matteo? I'll be there in about thirty minutes. Make sure that idiot builder is ready to explain how he plans to fix this." He ends the call without waiting for a response, and I wiggle my eyebrows.

"You're so sexy when you're demanding and forceful."

He's still frowning at his phone, and it seems to take him a second to absorb what I said. "What?"

"Never mind. We can role-play later. You can be the dynamic, impatient architect, and I'll be the incompetent builder you need to fuck into compliance."

He blinks in bemusement but doesn't object. "Whatever you want. Are you ready?"

I wave my phone with the list at him. "Yep!"

Micah puts his arm around me like he always does, and the world spins away, reforming into my entry hall. I guess this is the only part of my house he's seen. I'll give him the grand tour later, but for now, he has a builder to intimidate.

"I shouldn't be long," he assures me. "And I'll bring lunch when I come back. Anything in particular that you're in the mood for?"

"Mm, a sandwich from that place in Zurich Garrett was

talking about would be good." I've wanted one ever since he told me how amazing they are.

Micah cracks a smile. "How do you know it would be good when you've never had one?" he teases.

I pout. "Garrett made it sound like the best sandwich ever. Isn't it?"

"No, it is. I just like messing with you." He leans down to kiss me. "Get started, and I'll be back as soon as I can." He teleports out.

With a little sigh—we've barely ever been apart for weeks now, and I miss him already—I turn and look down the hallway. The house is a little musty from being closed up, and the first thing I do is open the front door. I probably shouldn't— even though the neighbors look out for me, a wide-open door in a neighborhood like this is an invitation to be robbed—but I want some cross flow of air. And it's a gorgeous early spring day outside. A month ago, I might have thought it was on the chilly side, but given that we're still getting regular snowfall in Hortplatz and will be for a couple more months, my assessment of "chilly" has changed.

I go into the living room and open the blinds and windows there, flooding the room with light and fresh air. Then I move steadily through the small house, doing the same in every room. I'm not sure yet what I'll do with the house—my instinct is to put it on the market now, but the sensible part of me thinks it would be wise to wait for six months and see if I'm still happy in Hortplatz. (I will be, of course. Micah's amazing. Duh.) It can't hurt to wait, and I guess I can rent it or something in the meantime?

I make a mental note to look into that later. Maybe call a realtor over lunch.

Next, I head for the kitchen and grab a water bottle. Micah gets upset whenever I mention that before him, I'd forget about things like food and water, so I'm going to impress him with how hydrated I am when he gets back. Or at the very least, he'll see the still-full water bottle and know I tried.

In my workroom, I turn a full circle, taking in the organized chaos. It looks wrong, probably because most of my everyday tools are in Hortplatz and there are gaping spaces where they usually live. Maybe I should start in the bedroom. I definitely could do with some more clothes—I never thought I'd care about what I wear, but after washing and re-wearing the same two sets of clothes for over a month, I'm ready for a change.

Abandoning the workroom for now, I devote myself to going through my dresser and wardrobe for warm, comfortable clothes. And not-so-warm ones. The weather in Hortplatz will improve eventually.

I'm interrupted by a shout from the front of the house, and I go to see who it is. Lenny, my neighbor across the street who does sketchy things, is hovering in the doorway.

"Hi," I say brightly. "How've you been?"

"Can't complain." He's frowning at me, but frowns don't bother me anymore, after over a month of living in the frowniest place on Earth. "You just get in?"

"Yep! But I'm not staying. My boyfriend's coming soon to help me pack some stuff."

An eyebrow shoots up. "That where you've been? We wondered. What's this boyfriend like? He good to you?"

"The best," I assure him happily. "Treats me like a god. *And* he's got crazy good reflexes. I hardly ever knock into things or trip when he's around."

Lenny's face softens. "Good. You need someone to fuss over you. Listen, there's this dude been hanging around your place. Was coming by a coupla times a week until me and the boys had a chat with him. I haven't seen him for a while, but it might be good if you're somewhere else for a bit. I didn't like his vibe."

This sounds like something I should worry about, but I'm not. With my tools in Hortplatz, there's nothing in the house really worth stealing. "Did he try to break in or something?"

"Nah." Lenny shakes his head. "Just stared at the house. Pounded on the door a few times, but when I asked if he wanted me to pass a message, he said no."

I don't blame the stranger. I'm pretty sure Lenny wasn't wearing a welcoming smile when he offered.

"Okay, well, me and my favorite stuff will be somewhere else for a while. If he does break in, call me so I can come and do all the... stuff." What *do* you do when someone breaks in? I guess some people would call the authorities, but around here, that's just a waste of time. Insurance people? Only my tools are insured. If a window or door is broken, I'll have to fix that to stop animals and squatters from wandering in.

It might just be easier to rent the place. "You know anyone who wants a short-term rental?" I ask Lenny. I don't know why I didn't think of this before. He'd make sure anyone he recommended was respectful of my property.

He purses his lips and looks toward the ceiling. "Maybe. The sister of a friend just left her shitty husband. She and her kid are crashing with my friend right now, but there's not a lot of room. She's only there because we're all worried the dickwad's gonna come after her." He rubs the back of his neck. "But if she was here, with me right across the street... maybe."

"Her husband was abusive?" My hackles rise. Nobody should ever be in a position where they're afraid to live alone. "If she wants it, she can have it, rent free." He frowns, and I add quickly, "I don't want it empty, and who knows what kind of tenants I'd end up with otherwise? I'd rather have someone I can trust to look after the place." Never mind that I've never met her and wouldn't recognize her walking down the street. Lenny knows her, and that's good enough for me.

He still doesn't look completely happy, but he nods. "I'll call, see what she thinks. Meanwhile, you oughtta keep this door shut, man. You don't have a screen or anything. Anyone can just walk in."

"I'll close it now," I promise. "I just wanted to air the house out a bit, get rid of the empty smell, you know?"

He pats me on the shoulder. "You're good people, Cam. I'll come over later when your boyfriend is here, say hello. Make sure he knows he's gotta treat you right."

I almost grin at the thought of Lenny facing down Micah, who might be my teddy bear but is still damn intimidating to others. "For sure," I agree. "You'll love him."

Lenny mutters his goodbyes over his shoulder as he walks out, and I dutifully close and lock the door behind him. Dropping the keys into their bowl on the hall table, I make for my workroom. Sure, there's still a pile of clothes on the bed to be dealt with, but I kinda just remembered that I didn't bring my suitcase with me. So until Micah gets here and can go get it for me, I'm just organizing things.

I start by going through my workbench, grabbing all the extra bits and tools I don't use very often but that can come in handy for specialist work. I arrange them neatly in groups by weight and shape, which will make a difference when packing them. Trust me on this—you don't want to put all your heaviest stuff in the same bag. You especially don't want to then drop said bag on your foot. Ask me how I know.

Once I'm sure there's nothing else on the workbench that needs to be packed, I head for the closet. I converted one side into shelf storage a while back, because I didn't need to hang clothes or anything in there. The other side is where I keep the stick vacuum and broom and stuff. Those can probably stay for my tenant, since the house in Hortplatz already has them. I'm gonna need my workbench, though. I wonder how much I'll need to bribe Micah's cousins to teleport it. That bitch is heavy.

I swing the closet open and stumble back a step before my brain even processes what I'm seeing.

A man.

With a knife.

Lunging at me.

# CHAPTER TWENTY-NINE

## Micah

To say I tore that builder a new one would be understating it. When I got there and saw what he'd done—which turned out not to be due to incompetence, but rather his notion that he knew better than me—I channeled Grandmother and ripped him to shreds... figuratively.

Then, fueled with self-righteous victory, I went to Garrett's favorite sandwich shop in Zurich and ordered lunch for me and Cam. I even got some pastries for dessert, since I earned the sugar and fat by facing down the evil know-it-all builder and giving up time with Cam. I could have been helping him pack up his house like a supportive boyfriend, and instead I had to work. Though, if I'm completely honest, packing up his house doesn't sound like the most fun way for us to spend the afternoon, and I'm not all that sorry I missed part of it. Maybe he's gotten enough done that we can take a break and test if his mattress is better than mine. It's the responsible thing to do, right? Spinal posture while sleeping is very important.

I'm mentally rehearsing the argument I'll use to convince him of that as I teleport into his front hallway, laden down with paper bags from the sandwich shop. I know immediately that Cam's not there.

Shaking my head, wondering if the teleport somehow messed up my senses—which is impossible—I call, "Cam?"

He's been here; I'd know that even if I hadn't brought him here myself. I can smell him, both the layers of residual scent that built up over the years of him living here and the new, fresh scent from today. I might not be a hellhound, but this kind of scenting is well within my limits. He was here in the hall—someone else was too, though they stayed right near the front door, I think. Their scent isn't in the hallway, exactly. Could someone have knocked? One of Cam's neighbors, maybe? He might have gone to one of their houses to collect his mail or something.

Before I go knocking on people's doors in search of him, I'll check the rest of the house. Maybe he left a note. Or he could be out the back? I'm pretty sure he has a small yard.

I go into each room, looking for signs of his presence. The air is much fresher than when I dropped him off, and I find a trail of open windows to support that. He's been in every room, including the kitchen, where I leave our food on the counter. The back door is open, and I stick my head out. His yard is more a courtyard, concreted over like the front and completely barren. That doesn't surprise me—Cam would forget to take care of a garden, then get upset when it died.

But where is he?

I'm getting a vague hint of another person, but they didn't stay in the kitchen long enough for me to process their scent. I wish Garrett was here. Could this be the same person who was at the front door? Maybe I was wrong about them not coming inside.

There's a small second bedroom off the kitchen, and I head in that direction.

And freeze.

Some of Cam's tools are scattered on the floor.

There's no way he'd leave them like that. No way. His tools are his babies. I've watched him check and clean them enough times to know he would *never* leave them lying on the floor like this.

I fumble in my pocket for my phone even as I inhale deeply, trying to capture any hint as to what happened. There was someone else here, and they must have been here for a while, because their scent has puddled. That's good—that's going to help. And... what is that? It smells metallic, but... new? Could it be one of Cam's tools?

I hit the contact for Cam's phone, then turn in horror when it rings behind me. It's lying on the floor by the closet.

Time to call for help.

"Micah?" Garrett says into my ear. "I thought you and Cam were packing today."

"We are. Something's happened. I need your nose, now." There's a faint tremor in my voice, and I breathe deeply. I was hoping it would calm me, but all it does is draw more of the combined Cam/stranger scent into my nostrils.

"Are you okay? Hold on, I'm getting Zac."

Fuck. I forgot he's at the cave with Zac and Ronan. No, wait... he can't be at the cave, or the call wouldn't have gone through. I probably should have called Gideon, anyway. He's the one with Enforcement contacts.

I open my mouth to tell Garrett not to worry, when my gaze catches on Cam's workbench. Or, more specifically, on the gleam of red blood on the corner.

*No.*

"Micah? Micah!" Zac's yelling in my ear, and I force myself to focus. Cam needs me.

"I'm here. I think Cam's been kidnapped."

There's a pause while Zac probably wonders why anyone

would kidnap a man who makes puzzles. I don't know, and I don't care. I just want him back.

"Send me a location picture," my cousin says, proving that he's got my back even when he's not sure what the fuck is going on. "We're coming."

I disconnect the call, step back into the kitchen, and snap a picture of the counter with our sandwiches on it. I don't want them teleporting into the workroom and potentially messing up evidence.

Only seconds after I send the text, I feel the tingle of an incoming teleport and Zac and Garrett appear in the middle of the kitchen. Garrett takes a moment to orient himself, then inhales deeply. "Human," he declares. "Male. Fully mature, I think. Cam was here too. Neither of them spent long in this room, though."

Silently, I point toward the workroom, and Garrett heads in that direction. "Call Ronan and tell him we're not coming," he says over his shoulder to Zac. "And let Asher know what's happening. And you should probably call Gideon or Alistair. If a human took Cam, we're going to need CSG's help."

"I'll call Gideon," I tell Zac, incredibly grateful that we have an in at the highest level of government. I don't think I could handle dealing with some random Enforcement officer right now.

My cousin answers his phone on the first ring. "Micah, I'm busy. I'll call—"

"Cam's been kidnapped by a human," I blurt, and Gideon stops midsentence.

"How is that possible? The roads are closed."

I shake my head, even though he can't see it. "No, we're at his place. We were going to pack his stuff. I had to leave for a while, and now he's gone. Garrett can smell a human here, and there's Cam's blood." The words come out in a jumble.

"A human?" Gideon's voice sharpens, then becomes muffled as he says to someone else, "Where's Alistair?"

Garrett comes back out of the workroom, his face grim. "Don't freak out, Micah, but Cam's injured."

Even though I already knew that, I still feel the blood drain from my head. Zac's hand clamps onto my shoulder, and I turn to see his concerned gaze on me, even as he talks into the phone held to his ear.

"Micah?" Gideon barks, grabbing my attention.

"Yes. Garrett says Cam's injured."

"Send me a location pic," my cousin orders. "I'll be there in ten minutes. Stay where you are—we don't need trouble with the humans."

Before I can retort that a human kidnapping my boyfriend means we *already* have trouble with them, he ends the call. I send him the picture of the kitchen counter, and then Zac, Garrett, and I retreat to the hallway to wait.

It feels endless.

Garrett sniffs. "Is that human?" He strides toward the front door, and I remember what I smelled earlier.

"Is it the same one?" I trail after him as he throws open the door, but he shakes his head.

"No, definitely not. Still human, still male, still mature, but not the same." He steps onto the front porch. "I can—" He breaks off suddenly, his gaze turning toward the street, and I look in that direction too. A man is crossing, eyes on us.

"Hey," he calls as he reaches the sidewalk and starts up Cam's little path. "One of you must be Cam's boyfriend."

Hope lights me up. "That's me. Do you know where he is?" Maybe he hit his head accidentally and went to his neighbors for help.

The man reaches the bottom of the porch steps and stops. "What do you mean? He's not here?"

The hope drains away, and my shoulders slump. "No."

"I'm Garrett," Garrett says, holding a hand out to the man, who comes up the porch steps to shake it. "This is Micah. He was supposed to meet Cam, but he's not here."

"Lenny," the guy says, jerking a thumb toward his chest. "He was here an hour ago. I came over to tell him off for leaving the front door open. People like Cam—he's quiet, you know? Good neighbor—and I try to keep an eye out, but this still isn't the greatest neighborhood. He asked if I knew anyone who wanted to rent his place, and I know he locked the door when I left."

"It was locked when I opened it just now," Garrett confirms, and Lenny gives him an odd look.

"How'd you get in?"

"Back door," I mutter, not really listening. The other human must have come through the back door. That's why I only smelled him in the kitchen. There's a gate from Cam's yard to the alley, isn't there? I'm sure I saw one, though I wasn't paying much attention.

Lenny's mouth is set in a firm line. "Something about this is wrong," he declares. "Cam was looking forward to you coming. You tried calling him?"

"His phone's here." I'm not sure how much to tell Lenny —he might want to call the human police, and that would be a disaster—but the sound of footsteps interrupts us in any case. I look over my shoulder into the house to see Gideon and Alistair coming down the hall, followed by Zac. Alistair's face is unusually grim, and it makes him look different.

"Full house," Lenny says, sounding a little suspicious.

"My cousins." I point them out. "And this is—"

"I know you. Cam's friend. You've been here before."

Alistair nods curtly. "You live across the street, right? Seen anyone hanging around?"

Lenny's face goes hard. "You think someone took Cam?

Fuck. It was probably that creep who's been watching his house. I told Cam about him, but he brushed it off."

"Someone was watching his house?" Gideon and Zac say it in unison. Alistair's breathing deeply, which I know means he's smelling for stuff. Garrett told me his cousin has had some pretty intense training in scent tracking and can process smells in a way most people don't believe is possible.

But my mind is joining dots. "His stalker. It's got to be him. I... Where's Cam's phone?" I start to push past my cousins to go back inside, but Gideon stops me and silently hands over Cam's phone. I unlock it with shaking hands, grateful that Cam gave me the code one time, and open his texts. "Here." I give it back to Gideon. He's the expert here. "The guy bought a puzzle, filed a chargeback before it shipped, then went ballistic when he didn't get the puzzle and Cam reported him for fraud. He's been sending harassing texts and emails ever since, even though Cam keeps blocking him."

Gideon scrolls through the texts. I don't know why Cam never deleted them, but that's got to be good now, right? We can use them to find him... right? Finally, Gideon looks up and exchanges a glance with Alistair, then turns to Lenny. "Can you describe the man who's been watching the house? Tall, short—"

"Man, I can do better than that. I got a picture." He hauls out his phone, taps the screen a few times, swipes, then holds it out. We all lean in to look. The man on the screen is in profile, standing in front of Cam's house. It's hard to tell from the image, but he looks to be tall, medium build. White, dark hair, average features. But I recognize him.

"That's the guy who was knocking when I came to get Cam the first time." I explain how he ran off when I arrived. "I wouldn't have remembered him, but it was weird."

"Can I text this to myself?" Gideon asks Lenny.

"Knock yourself out."

When Gideon hands the phone back, he looks Lenny in the eye. "Thanks for your help. We've got this from here."

Lenny, unsurprisingly, appears intimidated, but he squares his shoulders. "You boys connected?"

Gideon says nothing, but Alistair smiles. It's not nice. He doesn't look like himself at all.

Nodding slowly, Lenny says, "My kid is home, so I gotta sit this out. But call if you need anything. Cam's good people."

"Thank you," I tell him, feeling guilty for the assumptions I made about him when I first met Cam.

He gives me an up-nod, then turns and walks back across the street. "What's the plan?" I ask quietly. "Did you find anything?"

"I've got their scent," Alistair says as he leads us back inside. "They went out through the back gate. There was a car waiting."

My heart sinks, but neither Gideon nor Alistair seem worried.

"Can you track that?" I ask hopefully, and the big hell-hound nods.

"No problem. But if you know this guy's name, we might be able to get an address even faster."

I shake my head. "Cam never said. It's probably in his computer somewhere, but I wouldn't know where to look."

Gideon squeezes my arm. "If the scent trail craps out, we'll give that a shot, but let's see what Alistair can do first." Back in the kitchen, he stops to give orders. "Asher and Garrett are staying here in case Cam manages to get away and comes back. Micah, Zac, you'll come with us. You'll stay out of Alistair's way and do as you're told."

Zac opens his mouth to protest, and I shove him. He'll do what it takes to get Cam back, *or else*.

Alistair nods. "Let's go."

# CHAPTER THIRTY

## Cam

The first thing I become aware of is the pain in my head. Ow, ow, ow. What the fuck happened?

The second thing I become aware of is the man muttering to himself. Carefully, I slit one eye open, catch sight of the stranger pacing back and forth across the room, and close my eye again as memory floods back. Stranger with a knife in my closet, lunging at me. Me trying to get away but tripping over my own feet. My head hitting the workbench.

And then nothing.

Fuck.

One thing's for sure, this can't be good.

I'm not still in my house—I got that much from my brief peek. But I'm in *a* house, lying on what feels like a couch. Trying to be subtle, I shift my weight to see if my phone's still in my pocket. It's not... and I'm not subtle.

"Are you awake? You are! Open your eyes."

I don't want to, but I'm also really bad at faking sleep, so reluctantly, I open my eyes and sit up.

Mistake.

The room spins around me, and I clamp a hand to my aching head and moan.

"I didn't hit you!" the stranger yells. "I didn't! It's not assault. They can't arrest me."

I'm pretty sure the fact that he was hiding in my closet with a knife means he can be arrested, but whatever.

"Please stop yelling," I whimper, and he falls silent. "Where am I?" Maybe if I play dumb, he'll... what? Let me go? I don't know why he took me in the first place.

"Safe," he insists. "You're somewhere safe."

That's not as reassuring as he seems to think.

"Everything's going to be fine," he continues. "Once you're finished, you can go home."

...what?

Once I'm *finished?*

"Once I'm finished what?" The throbbing in my head eases from kill-me-now to you'll-die-later, and I cautiously lower my hand to look at the stranger. He's completely unremarkable apart from the slightly crazed expression and the fact that he's sweating profusely. I definitely don't feel safe.

"My puzzle. I ordered it, and you never sent it. That's bad customer service."

I blink several times, not sure what the fu—

"Wait... Cary? Are you Cary Mack?" No way has this guy kidnapped me because I wouldn't give him something he didn't pay for. *No way.*

Except I'm pretty sure that's exactly what happened.

"Yeah," he says, confirming my hunch. "I've been texting and emailing for years, and you're ignoring me. You can't ignore me now. I need my puzzle."

"You didn't pay for the puzzle," I point out. "So it's not yours." I don't tell him that it actually belongs to a dragon now. He wouldn't believe me if I did.

"That's not how it works," he snaps, and I give up all hope of reasoning with him. Because that is, in fact, how it works, and if he won't even admit that, logic isn't going to work.

"What time is it?" I ask. He looks confused by the sudden change in subject, but glances at his watch.

"Two-fifteen."

Micah will be back by now and know I'm missing. That's good. I just need to keep this idiot from hurting me until I'm rescued. Hopefully, that'll be soon.

Except... I don't want to be rescued. Why do I always need other people to rescue me? Fuck that noise.

Slowly, trying not to make my head hurt more than it does already, I get off the couch and stand straight. Ouch.

"I'm leaving now," I announce.

Cary's jaw drops. "What? No!" he sputters. "You can't leave! You need to make my puzzle."

"I really don't. I'm tired of being stepped on by spoiled, entitled fools who think they have the right to anything from me. You had the chance to own one of my puzzles, and you tried to steal it from me. Worse, you tried to damage my business reputation while you were at it. That's not okay, and I'm not putting up with it anymore." I take two shaky steps toward the door.

With a wordless shriek, he produces the knife from somewhere and races toward me. I sigh. "Stop that now," I say, unleashing my enthrallment ability. It's the first time in my life I've ever used it *against* someone, instead of as a mutually agreed-upon sex toy. Power flows through me, rolling into my voice, and Cary stumbles to a halt.

Whoa. It's never been that effective before. Maybe because Cary is human?

Whatever. This is my chance to leave. "Put the knife on that table," I suggest, gesturing, and he does, keeping his eyes on me, eager to do anything I want. I feel sick, knowing how easy this kind of power would be to pervert. "Now sit on the couch, there. Make yourself comfortable and stay there until someone comes to get you." I put a bit of extra emphasis behind that one. The power of my suggestions will start to wear off when I leave, and it would be great if he was still here when I send Enforcement to find him. I'm not sure what the exact process is when one enthralls a human, but I'm guessing they'll want to make sure he doesn't remember any of it. And I definitely want the stalking to stop. No more kidnappings, please.

He settles onto the couch and pulls his legs up, and I back slowly toward the door. He stays put, though his pleading gaze follows me until I turn away and can't see it anymore.

In the hallway, I make the decision not to go out the front door. Instead, I go in search of a phone. I need to call for a ride... and backup. But if Cary has a phone, it's on him, and I don't want to deal with him anymore. Instead, I go through the door off the laundry room into the garage. There's a car parked there with the back door still open—I guess that's how he got me here. I peer inside and grin. It's also how I'm going to leave.

I slam the back door, then get into the driver seat, where Cary has so thoughtfully left the key in the ignition. The car even has an in-dash GPS, which is going to make getting home nice and easy. And then Micah will find me, and I can collapse into his arms and let him take care of the rest. Poor Micah. He must be so worried about me by now.

I start the car, program in my destination, and find out I'm only ten minutes from home. Creepy. I'm pretty sure that when Cary originally placed his order, the shipping address wasn't this close—I usually remember when they're in my neck of the woods. Did he move here to be closer to me?

A chill runs down my spine. Definitely time to leave.

I find the garage door opener behind the sun visor and

press the button. The door ponderously rises, and I tap the steering wheel impatiently. I'm tired, my head is killing me, and I miss my demon. I don't have time to wait.

Finally the door is open enough for the car to get through, and I put it in gear and ease my foot onto the accelerator.

I'm halfway down the short driveway when a hellhound bounds into my path and growls. I hit the brakes, jolting against the seat belt, and joyful relief floods me as I recognize him.

Turning off the car, I scramble out. Alistair's on me before I'm clear of the door, jumping up to lick my face. He won't shift back out in the open like this, where he might be seen, but just knowi—

"Cam!"

The shout has me spinning—and then my head continues to spin, but I ignore it and stumble down the driveway toward Micah. He closes the distance between us in a few huge strides, then closes me into his arms.

And finally, everything's okay.

I rest my head on his chest and let all my worries go. Micah's here, and he'll fix everything. Tears of relief rise, but I blink them away.

"Are you okay?" he murmurs, his face buried in my hair. "I swear, if he hurt you—"

"I'm okay." It's barely a whisper, but he hears me. "I tripped when he startled me and hit my head, but he didn't do anything else." I draw back and look up at him. "You were right—about me needing to call Enforcement about my stalker customer. It was him."

"We know. Lenny said he's been watching your house."

Oh. Huh, that does make sense. Too bad I didn't think of it earlier when Lenny mentioned it.

"Where is he, Cam?" Gideon, the scary cousin, asks. I can

tell he's trying to sound gentle, but he fails. Good thing I'm not a delicate flower.

I point back toward the house. "He should be on the couch in the living room, but he might not be. I enthralled him to get away. Am I in trouble? He had a knife."

Gideon shakes his head. "Even if he didn't, you wouldn't be in trouble. He kidnapped you. You're within your rights to use your abilities to regain your freedom. Is he injured?"

"No." I shake my head quickly, then wince.

"Then we'll just need a statement from you later. I'll come to Hortplatz to get it, if I don't have time while you're with the healer."

"So I can take him home?" Micah... well, it's phrased like a question, but it sounds like a demand.

"Healer first," Gideon reminds him. "There still isn't one in Hortplatz, right?"

"We're working on it," Zac says. "Can you recommend someone here?" He eyes Micah warily.

Alistair whines, and Gideon glances toward the house. "Yeah. Sit in the car and wait for us. We'll secure Cam's kidnapper and hand him over to the team that deals with humans, and then I'll take you to the healer."

Micah tenses, like he's going to protest the wait, but I pat his chest. My head hurts, sure, but it's not life-threatening. I can wait a bit.

In his arms, I can wait forever.

ᛗ

Later, I snuggle back into his arms in our bed in Hortplatz. I've never been so grateful to be home ever.

"You know what I realized today?" I murmur, and he kisses the top of my head.

"What?"

"I can look after myself."

"I already knew that. You can do anything."

I smile at the way his voice rings with sincerity. A man who believes in me—my dream come true. "Yeah, but even though I can do it myself, I like that you want to do it for me sometimes. Like... I didn't want to spend even one more second with Cary Mack, so I rescued myself, but I loved being able to hand over the rest to you and be taken care of. I —" Huh. I pause and process the words that want to roll off my tongue. "I love you."

He stills, then shifts up onto one elbow so he can see my face. "You sound surprised by that."

I sit up and shrug, then crawl into his lap. "I am, I guess. Not that I could be in love with you—I knew that would happen. But it happened really fast."

He buries his face in my hair and inhales deeply, taking in my scent. "Not as fast as it did for me."

Wha—

I tip my head back to meet his gaze. "You love me?"

Micah nods. "With everything I am."

Home suddenly has a new meaning. It's here, with Micah and love.

🙟

Thank you for reading *Micah*! I hope you fell in love with him and Cam.

Next up is Zac and Ronan's book! You can grab *Zachary* here: https://readerlinks.com/l/3637268

If you don't know Ronan's origin story yet, I strongly recommend you read *Conspiracy of Dragons*. You can find it here: https://readerlinks.com/l/2609010

We talk spoilers in my Facebook reader group, RoMMance
with Becca & Louisa.
Or you can subscribe to my newsletter to get all updates and
access to bonus scenes: https://bit.ly/LouisaMBonus.

For early access to chapters of my upcoming books, artwork,
and other bonus material, check out my Patreon here:
patreon.com/louisamasters

# ALSO BY LOUISA MASTERS

Saddles & Suits

Alistair's Extraordinaries

Grave Situation

Elemental Men: The Complete Series

*Style Me*

Rebrand

Couture

*Elf Magic*

Wooing the Wiccan

Enticing the Elf

*The Collective*

Higher Demon

Demon Hunter

*Demons-In-Law*

Asher

Micah

Zachary

*Franklin U*

Mr. Romance

The Holigay Hookup *related novella

Batting Style

*Ghostly Guardians*

Spirited Situation

Vortex Conundrum

Conduit Crisis

Gateway Catastrophe

*Here Be Dragons*

Dragon Ever After

The Professor's Dragon

The Dragon Experiment

Conspiracy of Dragons

*Hidden Species*

Demons Do It Better

One Bite With A Vampire

Hijinks With A Hellhound

Sorcerers Always Satisfy

Hidden Species Box Set

*Met His Match*

Charming Him

Offside Rules

A Christmas Chance (novella)

Between the Covers (M/F)

*Joy Universe*

I've Got This

Follow My Lead

In Your Hands

Take Us There

*Novellas*

Fake It 'Til You Make It (permafree)

One Golden Night

O Hell, All Ye Shoppers

Out of the Office

After the Blaze

Blokes Down Under Novella Collection

Louisa Masters started reading romance much earlier than her mother thought she should. As an adult, she feeds her addiction in every spare second. She spent years trying to build a "sensible" career, working in bookstores, recruitment, resource management, administration, and as a travel agent before finally conceding defeat and devoting herself to the world of romance novels.

Louisa has a long list of places first discovered in books that she wants to visit, and every so often she overcomes her loathing of jet lag and takes a trip that charges her imagination. She lives in Melbourne, Australia, where she whines about the weather for most of the year while secretly admitting she'll probably never move.

http://www.louisamasters.com